CAGE

(Corps Security, Book 2)

A novel by Harper Sloan

xoxo

D1410233

2

Copyright © 2013 by E.S. Harper.

Braxxon Breaker Dialogue, Copyright © 2013 Crystal D. Spears

All rights reserved.

ISBN 13: 978-1492375678

ISBN 10: 1492375675

No part of this book may be reproduced or transmitted in any form or by any means, electronic or mechanical, including photocopying, recording, or by any information storage and retrieval system without the written permission of the author, except for the use of brief quotations in a book review.

This book is a work of fiction. Names, characters, places, and incidents, either are the products of the authors imagination or are used fictitiously. Any resemblance to actual persons, living or dead, events, or locations is entirely coincidental.

All rights reserved. Except as permitted under the U.S. Copyright Act of 1976, no part of this publication may be reproduced, distributed, or transmitted in any form or by any means, or stored in a database or retrieval system, without the prior express, written consent of the author.

This book is intended for mature adults only.

Cover Art Designed by Indie Pixel Studio

Editing by Katie Mac

Interior Design by MGBookCovers

Acknowledgments

Crystal Spears, my soul sister! Meant to be baby! Thank you for everything you have done, everything you will do, and for being you. I consider myself one lucky bitch to have you in my life!

Katie Mac, I can't thank you enough… well, I can. You are the best and I am one blessed chick to be a part of your kickass 'family'!

My badass betas! Danielle, Debi, Amber, Elle, Angela, and Becky. I am convinced I have the best betas In. The. World. You girls, you know exactly what I need to hear and when it needs to be said. You know how to tell me with love that the direction I went wasn't so good. And you love my men fiercely. I LOVE YOU ALL!

Danielle Calcote…this is my promise in writing. The beast is yours. Enjoy him!

Debi Barnes…Shauna misses Gina. I love you my minion lover!

Amber Vaughn… I love you. Seriously. Lady boner in full salute to your awesomeness.

Elle Wilson…girl, you know exactly what I need to say and how to say it. From now on if I doubt myself I know who to call!

Angela Lane… best brainstorming partner ever! You find the holes and help me fix them! <3

Becky Schmidt… I love you, your megaphone and your love for me. LOL! Cheers to having me rolling in laughter with all the comments we had rocking!

Katie, Kelly, and Angela. The girls that keep me going, keep me entertained, and make sure I haven't locked myself in a dark room. You girls have been by my side since Corps Security was just a thought. I would, without a doubt, be lost without y'all!

Brenda, I have been so lucky to have you in my life during this journey. Your messages and texts never fail to bring a smile to my face. For taking the formatting nightmare off my hands, and being the best damn pimp I ever did meet!

Chelcie! I love you. You know this, but just in case you forgot… you are one sexy bitch!

JB, thank you for making two of the most beautiful covers, and for putting up with my crazy!

Melissa Gill-I love you! Like really. My Swag Slinger. My graphic queen. I am so glad that we have become great friends!

To my street team AND my babes! Believing in me, my boys and pimping me hard! BEST LADIES EVER!

Each and every reader, reviewer, blogger, fan. This wouldn't be anything without you. I wouldn't be living my dreams without the support that you have given me. Your messages, comments and reviews make this worth it. I love you all.

To the dentist and hygienist and ladies over at Vassey Dental. (A big shout out to Dr. Harrah and Dr. Naik. Michele and Phyllis.) Without your torture **kidding** I doubt I would have these books done right now. No one likes going to the dentist, but I love going to mine!

CAGE PLAYLIST

Sam Grow- Lay You Down
One Republic- I Lived
Luke Bryan-Country Girl (Shake it for me)
Buckcherry- Crazy Bitch
Robin Thicke- Blurred Lines
Daft Punk ft Pharrell Williams- Get Lucky
Walk Off the Earth- Red Hands
Will.i.am ft Brittany Spears- Scream & Shout
Flo Rida- Good Feeling
My Darkest Days- Casual Sex
Taylor Swift- Everything Has Changed
Boys Like Girls- Two is Better than One
P!nk- The Great Escape
Hunter Hayes- I Want Crazy
Josh Turner- Time is Love
Christina Aguilera- Fighter
ACDC- You Shook Me All Night
The Band Perry- If I Die Young
Mariah Carey- #Beautiful
Foghat- I Just Wanna Make Love To You
Sarah McLachlan- Angel
Plain White T's- Rhythm of Love
The Black Keys- I'll Be Your Man

Dedication:

To my parents.
For teaching me to dream and showing me how.
Love you both.
More than you will even know.

And to my Dad.
First man I ever loved and ½ of my biggest
cheerleading duo.
For supporting me and pushing me to be the
greatest I can be.

Disclaimer:

This book is not suitable for younger readers. There is strong language, adult situations, and some violence.

To contact Harper:
Email: authorharpersloan@gmail.com
Facebook:
www.facebook.com/harpersloanbooks
Goodreads:
www.goodreads.com/harper_sloan
Twitter: @harpersloan
Instagram: @harper_sloan

Prologue

"Greg Cage." I bark into my phone. I've been sitting outside of the damn ultrasound place for the last thirty-minutes. Of course, the actual parents are running late. Those two can't keep their hands off of each other.

God, I want that.

"Hello?"

"Yeah, Cage. It's Derrick." The knot in my stomach grows. This motherfucker has been nothing but a headache for the last two years.

"News?" I don't have time for this bullshit today.

"Um, yes?"

"Derrick, I do *not* have the patience for this right now. You called me for a reason, and I swear to Christ, it better be a good one. Has that slimy motherfucker finally slipped up?" I've had Derrick, a local cop, keeping tabs on my ex-brother-in-law for the last two years, ever since Simon married another innocent woman. I know there is something going on there, but I haven't been able to get a speck of dirt on that asshole. Grace would be sick if she knew how deep my need for vengeance runs.

"Um, yeah... that's why I'm calling, Cage. I just don't know how you're going to handle this news." Derrick might be a stand up kind of guy, but in times like this, I just want to punch him in his pretty boy face.

"What. Is. It?" I see Axel's truck pulling into the parking lot, and I know I need to be off this phone before Izzy sees me. I love her, but the second she senses my stress, she won't stop until she has some answers. I refuse to cloud her happiness right now.

"It's about his wife Sofia. Well, you see... there was an accident last night."

"Fuck..." I hiss.

Just like Grace. Just like my beautiful sister.

"Please fucking tell me that there is something that ties his ass to this." There has to be. The coincidence is just too fucking much.

"That's just it. The accident. I wasn't on call last night, so this is all second hand until I get into the station...shit." I know this won't be good, I just know it. "Sofia made it long enough to be transported, but they called it shortly after she arrived at the hospital." He talks a deep breath before continuing, the whole time my stomach turning to stone. "She was DOA, Cage."

I see Izzy's big, blinding smile through the window of the car, and my heart lightens a little.

"I need to go. You keep me fucking posted. I don't mean every now and then either. I want to know every fucking detail, you got that?"

"Yeah, Cage. I understand."

When I hear him click off the line, I shove my phone in my pocket and get ready to greet Izzy. I see her walking up to me, her small stomach rounded with her progressing pregnancy. I can't help but smile.

The unease I feel from Derrick's call is still eating me but I shove it aside and wrap my arms around Izzy in greeting. "You ready, Baby Girl?" She looks up at me with the biggest smile, and I remember how easy it is for her to be so important to me. Grace would have loved her.

Her blinding smile, so full of love and happiness helps to wipe away all the webs of distress that have just fallen all over me.

Life moves on.

Now I just need to figure out how to forget that motherfucker Simon Wagner.

CHAPTER 1

(A little over a year later)

The sound of my headboard slapping heavy against the wall is almost loud enough to drown out the insistent ringing of my cell phone.

"Fuck," I snarl. Pulling my hand from the slender wrist I have bound behind this chick's back, I reach over and snatch the phone off my side table. "Don't speak." I bite out, feeling her pussy clamp tight around my dick. This chick loves when I boss her around.

"Cage," I answer, thrusting my hips forward and locking down hard. My breathing is coming in quick bursts, showing me just how hard I have been taking her. "Hello?"

"Uhh, G?" Izzy's soft voice comes through the line. Fuck. This is not how I need to answer the phone to her. She has been like my sister for the last four years.

"Yeah, give me a second, Baby Girl." Muting the phone, I pull my rock hard dick from Mandy's tight body and slap her ass, hard.

"Go get cleaned up. Play time is over." If looks could kill, I would be dead on the floor right now.

"Are you kidding me?" She rolls over, and with a huff, crosses her arms over her large and very fake tits.

"Not kidding, Mandy. Don't have time for your shit either. You know what this is, and I didn't make any promises earlier."

"Do you think that just once, you could actually act like you want me around?" She pouts.

I level her with a look of my own and roll off the bed, stripping my dick of the condom, and throwing it in the trash before walking out of the bedroom.

Once I get into the office, I unmute and take a deep breath before I speak. "Izzy, sorry. What's up?"

"I'm so sorry, G! I didn't think you would be... busy." I might have believed her if it weren't for her soft laughter.

"Funny. So? What's the early morning call for?"

"Okay, okay. Not laughing anymore. I need a huge favor. Nate's running a small fever, and I can't make his appointment. I need to meet with the wedding planner in an hour, and Ax is down at the office. I think he's just teething, but I would feel better with the wedding and all this weekend if I made sure. Anyway, I called Dee, but she can't take him because she has a meeting this morning, and

I tried Maddox because Ax said he was free, but he said 'no girl' and hung up on me... I think he has a friend over if you know what I mean." She isn't going to stop talking if I don't hurry this up. Izzy in 'frantic bride and worried mother' mode is just a hot mess.

"Iz, spit it out. If I can help, I will."

"Right. Can you take Nate to the doctor in an hour?"

"Yeah, Baby Girl. That wasn't that hard, was it now?"

She laughs before answering, but I can still hear the stress lacing her words. "Not hard, G. I feel like I'm losing my mind."

"Just hang in there. By the end of the weekend, everything will be worth it."

"I know, but I still feel like something is going to go wrong any second now."

"Stop stressing. Do you honestly think Axel would let anything stand in the way of making you his wife? Nope. Wouldn't happen. He would move mountains for you. Time to relax."

"All right, I'll try. Owe you one."

"No, you don't. You know I love spending time with little man. I'll swing by in about half an hour. Got some stuff I have to take care of here first."

"Oh, yeah... I can imagine." Her laughter is the last thing I hear before she disconnects.

When I turn around, Mandy is standing in the doorway, ass naked and scowl firmly in place.

"What?"

"Who the hell was that? You took a call when your dick was in my body. A call from another woman?"

Why do I put up with this bitch? Oh, that's right, because if I wait any longer to get some, my dick will shrivel off. "Amanda," I roar her full name. "Hear me right now. You do not get to sit here and sling that shit. My sister calls and I'm done. Get that now, if you ever plan on revisiting my bed."

"You're done? Your dick is still hard," she shrieks at me.

I don't have to look down to know that my dick is screaming at me to finish. I reach down and caress my balls, trying unsuccessfully to ease the ache that is coiling in my gut. *Fuck... I need this so bad.*

"Babe. I don't have time to take my time. You want to finish? Fine, but it will be hard and fast."

Her snarky mouth and creased brow immediately lift. The smile that takes over her face reminds me of why I waste my time with Mandy. She is fucking beautiful, and if I weren't such a cold bastard, I might want something more than a way to get my rocks off with her.

She saunters over to my desk and hops up on the edge, spreading her long, toned legs and revealing her wet pussy. "Come on baby. I'm dripping for you." She runs her red tipped fingernails along her folds, rubbing her clit a few times before pushing two fingers deep into her center. Sure enough, when she brings her digits out, they are gleaming with her juices.

"Want a taste, baby?" Her voice brings me back from my lust-induced fog, reminding me why she is here.

"Shut up." I growl before shoving my arms under her legs and lifting her pussy to my lips. She grabs hold of my hair, gripping it with her long fingers as I stand with her still attached to my mouth, eating like a starved man.

"Oh... Greg, baby! Love your mouth, love when you eat me."

I growl against her core, willing her to shut up.

Walking blindly back down the hall, I dip twice so that she doesn't knock her head against the door frame, and toss her back into the rumpled mess of my bed.

She quickly crawls over to the edge, and before I can stop her, my dick is all the way down her throat. I pause to enjoy her wicked fucking mouth for a second, and then I softly push her off me. "No time, Mandy. Got shit to do."

Reaching over to the side table, I grab another condom and roll it over my straining dick. *I'm going to blow a nut any second now if I don't get inside her body.*

"Roll over." She gives me another frown, but rolls over and pushes her ass high in the air. Grabbing one slim hip with my hand, I run the tip of my dick across her lips.

Every time the steel of my jewelry hits her clit, she wiggles impatiently.

"Fuck me!" She screams, pushing back with her hips.

"Better hold on Mandy. Going to take you hard." I ram into her pussy with one quick, deep thrust. She screams out in pleasure, rocking back to meet my forceful pounding. There is nothing loving about this; this is about a man and a woman meeting their needs.

It only takes a few minutes before her walls clamp tight on my dick, milking every last drop out of my body. With a firm slap to her cheek, I pull out and walk into the bathroom.

"Got to go, Mandy. Get ready. Time for you to take your fine ass home."

I shut the door just in time to miss whatever object she tosses across the room.

Crazy bitches. This is why I've avoided relationships for so long.

CHAPTER 2
Greg

Parking in front of Axel and Izzy's, I quickly jog up the steps and let myself in with my key. "Iz?" I call out, my voice echoing throughout the house.

"Back here, Greg. Just getting his bag ready for you." Assuming her voice is coming from the kitchen, I take off in that direction.

Turning the corner to the kitchen, I almost knock Izzy to the floor in her rushed flurry of activity. "Baby girl, you have got to calm down. What exactly do you think is going to happen, huh?"

"Oh, Greg… I don't know. I just feel like something is going to go wrong. Now with Nate sick, and the wedding this weekend, I just can't stop worrying."

"You need to chill. I promise you nothing is going to happen." I wrap her up in a hug, waiting for her frantic breathing to calm down a little. "Where's my little buddy for the day?"

"Over by the backdoor. He is obsessed with looking out the window right now." I walk off, letting her continue her rush around the kitchen.

Ah, there he is. The day that Nathaniel Gregory Reid was born was one of the best days of my life. Not because he is my child, no. Because the girl that has grown to be a sister to me not only gave birth to him, but she beat her demons and won in order to do so. Plus, it helps that the handsome little thing is named after his favorite uncle.

"Nate! How's the handsome baby boy today?" He turns from his window gazing and gives me a big, drooling smile. Scooping him up, I hold him close to my body, just enjoying the feel of his little body next to mine.

"Here's his bag. Snacks, sippy cup, and his paci. Diapers, wipes, and all the other things you might need. His appointment is with Dr. Shannon. You know how to get to the pediatrician's office, right?"

"Yeah, Izzy. I have this. I also have to go, or we will be missing that appointment. Want to trade cars so you don't have to switch out his seat?"

"That's fine, and Greg… thanks." She leans up and gives me a kiss on the cheek before smothering Nate in love. I might have even seen the poor kid begging me with his eyes to get him out of here. Uncle Greg to the rescue.

We make it to the doctor's office with minutes to spare. Getting Nate out of the car and into the office is the easiest part; trying to get my dog tags out of his mouth is a whole new issue. I know Izzy hates it when he does this to Axel, but damn, the poor kid is miserable. He goes from happy as hell to screaming in two seconds. I hate seeing little man in pain, so I know it has to kill Izzy and Axel.

Walking up to the sign in desk, I smile at the pretty little blonde. "Hello, I need to check in Nate Reid to see Dr. Shannon." She looks up at me, eyes wide, and I swear drool forms. I hate reactions like this. Yes, I am a large man, but damn. "Miss? Nate. To check–in."

"Oh, right. I'm sorry." She makes a few notes, looking up at me a couple times before blushing and almost shoves her head through her monitor. "Do you have your son's insurance cards? We just put a new system in, so we need to make sure they match."

The sharp pain that always comes crashing through my system at just the thought of having my own child never seems to dull. One day.

"Nate's my nephew. His mother, Izzy, didn't leave the cards, but I can assure you nothing has changed with their insurance." Since this little chick is still drooling, I'm guessing it's a safe bet she didn't hear a damn thing I just said. Looking down at her nametag I get ready to help her focus, scanning the basic script 'Lauren' before addressing her, "Lauren, darlin'?" She blinks a few times, and then finally gets with the program. She checks Nate in, and instructs me to have a seat to wait for someone to call us. Joy.

Following her instructions, I take Nate and plop down on one of the hard chairs in the waiting room. Jesus Christ, these things must be made for women or extremely small men. Adjusting Nate to make sure I can at least keep him happy and silent for the moment, I dig my phone out to send a quick text to Izzy to let her know we are here. Nate once again decides my tags make the best teething toys. Izzy can kick my ass, but there is no way in hell I will take those from him now that he is happy. Hell no.

Thirty minutes later and a soaked shirt, tags, and Nate, someone calls his name. "Nate Reid?" I hear the voice off to the side. Looking up, it's now my turn to swallow my tongue. Holy shit. It's been a while since just by looking at a woman knocked me on my ass. This is no ordinary woman. No, this woman screamed sex.

Her hot pink scrubs mold to her body as though custom made just for her. Maybe a good six inches under my six-foot-three, with legs so attractive that even her horrible uniform can't hide it, and tits… fuck me, those tits, huge. I have to force my tongue from darting out to lick my lips. Once I can finally remove my gawking eyes from her chest, I look up and meet the high arch of one dark brow and mocking blue eyes. Shit.

"Mr. Reid?" Damn, even her voice is sexy as hell. Low, raspy and even my dick takes notice.

I clear my throat before trusting myself to speak. "Cage."

"What?" Huh? Damn... what did I just say? *Cage.* Smooth, real smooth.

"Not Mr. Reid. I'm the uncle, Greg Cage." I feel like the teenage boy that just got his first boner for his best friend's mom. Could this get more awkward?

"Alright, Uncle Greg Cage, and how is this little guy today?"

I go to answer her, but before I can get the words out, Nate makes an odd sound deep in his throat. I register Nurse Wet Dream's gasp, and I step back right before Nate covers my whole body with his vomit. Way to help a man out, Nate.

After a ridiculously long and very uncomfortable doctor's visit, Nate is finally ready to leave. Izzy is going to freak. Double ear infection. The doctor explained that's the reason Nate so lovingly decided to cover me in his baby barf. And to make matters worse, I had to help hold the little guy down while the nurse stabbed his chunky little thigh with an antibiotic shot. I haven't seen the sexy as sin nurse since the doctor handed me Nate's prescriptions and walked off. I don't even realized that I don't know her name until I am walking Nate and his puke back out to the car. Well, *Nate* isn't rocking the foul smelling shit anymore.

Deciding it's best not let Izzy know just how sick Nate is, I drive down to the office to pass the little guy off to his father so that I can go home and shower. At least this way, if Sway comes out to attack me, I can protect myself with the shield of baby throw up.

"Ohhhhh!" I hear squealing like a damn pig before I can even climb out of Izzy's car. It's laughable that I think I might be able to avoid Sway. I swear that man never works, just sits by the window, and waits for someone from Corps to walk past or drive up.

"Gregory, get your fine ass over—THE BABY!" And now, I have Sway in all his glory running towards the car. How a man as round as him can run on four-inch heels without busting his ass is beyond me.

"No, Sway. Calm your ass down right now."

"Gregory, why are you all *wet*?" He pants, stopping as close as he can get without crawling into my body. I take a step back and shift Nate in my arms. Away from the deranged man.

"Would you please stop calling me *Gregory*? You sound like my damn mother." Sway reaches out, again, to take Nate from me. "No, Sway. Not today."

"But, Gregory!" He gasps and holds his beefy hand to his chest. Jesus.

"Got to run, Sway. You want to visit with the baby, then go attack Ax." I can hear Sway clicking behind me across the parking lot. This man, woman, whatever the fuck… I might give him a hard time but he is hilarious. "See you around, Dilbert!"

Walking into the office never fails to give me a massive sense of pride. Pride in myself, and pride in my boys. Before joining forces with Axel and the guys, I was doing pretty fucking hot by myself, but the more clients I picked up, the more overwhelming things got. Plus, that was when Izzy was going through so much shit… I just couldn't afford to be away that much. She needed me, and I will *never* fail another woman I love again.

Izzy and I have the best friendship. A lot of people think it is crazy, me being so close with a chick, but Izzy isn't just anyone to me. She is my blood… even when we aren't really. She holds just as big of a piece of my heart as Grace once did.

Damn, I miss Gracie.

"Hey, Greg." I hear a voice call softly from behind the reception desk.

"Emmy. How's it been around here, babe?"

"Everything's fine, Greg. Axel is running around like a mad man though. I think he's stressed about this weekend."

"I bet," I laugh, shifting Nate's body in my arms, "Got to go drop little man off. Not staying, but I'll see you this weekend."

"Alright, Greg." If I hadn't seen her bust one of the boy's balls over some shit, I would swear the timid little mouse is all weakness.

Shaking my head, I continue down the hall towards Axel's office. I can hear him booming orders through the closed door. Shit, someone must have seriously pissed him off this morning.

"Wouldn't do that if I was you." Turning around, I catch Beck's stoic face. Never good when this easy-going guy starts acting like a little bitch.

"Problem?"

"Yeah. About six and a half feet of pissed off. What the fuck is going on with him?" He reaches up and rubs his neck, another sure sign that Beck is stressing shit.

"My guess, the same thing that's eating Izzy. With all the shit they went through, they are both afraid to blink until the wedding is over." Damn shame too. Axel and Izzy don't have the fairytale beginning that most couples as perfect as them deserve. It might have taken them a while to reconnect, but they are worried for no reason. Not one of us would let anything happen to postpone this event.

"That all that's biting your ass today, Beck?"

"Just more shit with Dee. I don't know why I try so hard, I honestly don't." Looking closer, I notice the stress weathered all over his body. He is vibrating with frustration, and it is not a good look for him.

"What's the deal this week?" I ask, knowing damn well she has been giving him the run around for the better part of the last two years. I don't think anyone really knows what happened, but they went hard and heavy, then Dee put the brakes on real quick.

"Hell if I fucking know. Looks like she is bringing some tool from her office to the wedding. I don't know what the hell her issue is with just admitting we had something. I tell you this though; I am sick and tired of waiting for her to pull her thumb out of her ass."

"Right. Not getting in that shit. You might be my brother, but that chick will always out rank you." I turn and knock on Axel's door, not waiting for his reply before pushing our way through. Drama between Beck and Dee is nothing I want to dip my toes into. Hell no.

"What d—" Axel barks out before he realizes who is in his office.

"Nice douchebag. Your son decided to decorate me with his vomit today, so it's your turn. Love this boy, but I don't like smelling like your woman's tit milk."

"Why do you have my boy? Where is Iz? Is she okay?" He goes to get up, as if he is going to run out of the office to check on his woman. Damn, he is turning into a fucking pussy.

"Calm down. Jesus Christ. What is going on with you two? You're acting like a little bitch that just got her period, and she is on edge just waiting for the other shoe to drop. Nothing is going to happen, you feel me?"

He sighs and drops down heavy into his chair. "Yeah. I keep feeling like any second she is just going to disappear again, and nothing I do gets that image out of my mind. Not one damn thing." He shakes his head, collects his thoughts, and looks back at me. Determination blazes in his eyes. "Give me my boy, and don't cuss around him asshole."

"You're an idiot, Axel. Izzy is with the wedding something or other. Nate has been running a fever, so I just left the doctor. She didn't want to worry *you,* but serious as shit, right now there is no way I am taking him home and explaining all this to her when she is already freaking her shit."

"Yeah, she said something about him not feeling well last night, but he was happy when I left for work this morning. Is he okay? Dammit, why didn't she call me? You shouldn't have had to take my boy." He pulls Nate to his body and snuggles close. That ache in my heart stings a little deeper at the sight.

"I don't know, maybe because you've been acting just as bad as she has for the last two weeks. He's fine anyways. Ear infection, both ears. But I explained to the doc what the deal is with this weekend, so he gave him an antibiotic shot to speed shit up."

I toss Nate's prescriptions on the desk, kiss the little dude's head, and slap Ax on the back. "Buck up and calm the fuck down. Nothing is going to happen. But, if you can tell me the name of nurse sin, I'll give you a hundred bucks. Shit man."

Axel's laughter booms through the room, making Nate smile his toothy grin up at his father. "I know exactly who you are talking about, and if you tell Izzy I said this,

I'll cut your balls off, but damn… that woman. You see the size of her tits?"

"Hell, how could I miss them?"

We shoot the shit for a while before the smell of myself makes me want to add to the mess. Axel almost loses his shit again when I tell him what Izzy's phone call this morning interrupted. Axel has never been a fan of Mandy. He thinks she is a 'gold digging whore', and at this point, I can't say I disagree with him too much. Leaving the office, and having Emmy make sure the path from the door to my truck is Sway clear, I take off in hopes to clean off and relax for a few hours before something else is thrown in my lap.

CHAPTER 3
Melissa

Another long day I think will never end. Patients run over again, and Dr. Shannon refuses to close the doors until almost 8:30. I hate breaking plans with Cohen, but there is no way he will be able to go to dinner with me now. I fight the urge to punch a hole in the wall and continue my path to the bathroom, stripping the day's scrubs off on the way.

My mind wanders to the man who came in with Izzy's little boy today. He seemed like such a natural with Nate that it is obvious he has been around kids before, but Iz has never mentioned him. I had been lucky to strike up a friendship with Izzy West over the last ten months. When I first met her, I was on the other side of Dr. Shannon's door and coming in with Cohen instead of working. We struck up a friendship, and at the time, it was what I needed.

I remind myself to not to think about the events that led up to me becoming friends with Izzy. My sister would kick my ass if I shed one tear over her. No way. I've had my big girl panties on for over a year now and there is no damn way I would let memories pull me down.

Shaking off the pain that only comes when I look at Cohen's face, or think about my sister is the only reality I know right now. But I am damn good at it. I've dealt with losing my sister, but it doesn't make the pain vanish.

After my shower and nightly routine, I settle down on my worn couch and pick up the phone. It's time to check in with mom and face the music of missing out on another date with Cohen.

"Meli-Kate! You are in trouble my love. I had to explain, again, to Cohen that we can*not* use the kitchen table as a launching pad for his assault against the imaginary ninjas in the house! Do you know how long it takes to calm him down when there are imaginary ninjas attacking his Nana's house?"

I can't help the uncontrollable laughter that bubbles up at the thought of Cohen in attack mode. I know this will make for a lecture from my mother but damn, she is asking for it.

"Seriously mom! You make him sound like a terror! He isn't that bad!" I laugh at her. In reality, he really is that bad. We take care of Cohen, and have since my sister passed away almost two years ago. I miss her, but having him in our lives takes some of the sting away. It doesn't hurt that he keeps us on our toes so much that we don't have time to miss her as much.

"Meli," she sighs. "Please tell me there is a reason you missed your dinner with him again? You know how much he waits for these days." She sounds so broken, and I hate that I can't be there more for her and him.

"I know. Trust me, I do. Dr. Shannon did it again. They just kept coming, and there wasn't one damn thing I could do about it."

"Tomorrow. You're off, aren't you? Come over and get him tomorrow." She would have been able to play off the slight wobble in her voice if she hadn't cracked at the end, making my heart break. I know Cohen doesn't make things easy, but with me being the only one with a job, it is the only way we can make things work right now. Maybe one day I will have full custody of him, but with my sister's mother-in-law raising a stink about him, and fighting my sister's will, this was the way to play things right now.

"I can come early in the morning. I won't be able to keep him long though; I have the bachelorette party for one of my girlfriends tomorrow night. Remember? I told you I couldn't keep him this weekend?"

"Oh, that's right dear. It's okay, really. Janie down the street can always come and take him over to the park, and maybe fire some of that little boy energy right out of his ass." She snickers like always when a 'dirty word' leaves her mouth. My mother is the perfect example of a Southern Baptist woman. Growing up, all my friends said I was lucky as hell to have Paula Deen as my mom. It really is freaky how much she looks and sounds like that woman.

"I'll call you in the morning, okay? Just in case you change your mind. Love you mama."

"Love you too sweet child"

I hang up and the only thing I can think of is how lovely my twin bed will feel when I crash into it.

The next morning, the first thing I do is call my mom to see if she needs me to come take Cohen for a few hours. When I call though, Janie answers and says they are busy building forts in the living room and having popcorn wars. Sounds like the perfect day for me to be absent.

Since I'm not meeting up with Izzy and her friends until dinnertime, I spend the rest of the day cleaning my small one room apartment. Lucky for me, my apartment is so small it only takes me a few hours to have it perfectly spotless. Now, it's time to call Izzy.

"Hello?" The deep voice answering her phone throws me off for a second. I move the phone away from my ear to make sure I have the right number.

"Um, is Izzy available?"

"She sure is, but no way in hell is she able to talk right now." I hear Izzy protesting before she snatches the phone out of the man's hands and breathlessly speaks, "Hello?"

"Oh my God, Izzy! Please tell me I did not just interrupt you!"

"Seems to be the week for that." She giggles.

"Jesus Christ! I am so sorry! Just want to see what time I should meet you tonight?" Fuck me, perfect timing Melissa! At least someone is getting some these days! I will probably need to bust out the Swiffer to clean the cobwebs because it's been so long since my legs were spread.

"It's fine. Axel is just being a big baby, that insatiable man. Why don't you come over to the house and ride with me, Dee and Emmy?"

"Sounds perfect. See you then!" I hang up the phone and quickly go about getting ready for the night. I try my hardest to block out the tugs of arousal that pull at my skin. Lucky little bitch, damn I need to get laid.

My mind immediately comes back to 'Uncle Greg'; I know he is likely to show up at some point tonight. He wouldn't be at the doctor in Izzy's place if he weren't that close to them. So, the question is do I want to do anything with the attraction that simmers at a low boil just from a few seconds in the same room with him? No. Well, to be totally honest, I do, but I am smart enough not to get mixed up with someone so manly. After watching how well that turned out for my sister, there is no way I am getting involved with Mr. Sex on Legs. I need to find a short, skinny, balding man. Someone safe.

I might be many things, but I am also smart enough to learn from the past. Smart enough to know that no man who oozes so much alpha male will be happy with a woman who isn't weak. Or, he won't settle until he makes me weak, and I will *never* be that bitch.

Whichever way I slice it, I still can't ignore the way that just thinking about his devilishly sexy good looks and those eyes, fuck those eyes, turn me on like flipping the switch.

Getting out of the shower, and continuing the process of getting ready still has me pondering what I want to do with all this pent up attraction. I stand in the middle of my 'closet', actually a corner of my bedroom crammed with my clothing obsession, and debate between casual or sexy. Hey, I might have decided to stay away, but you never know what could happen. It's better to be prepared for anything.

I finally settle on one of my new dresses. Not the sexiest thing I own, but it shows off enough skin that it will be perfect. The deep green, halter style dress fits tight across my chest, and the V is deep enough that my girls will be on display. Let's face it; I know they are one of my best features, so why not show them off? The dress hangs loose, with one of those funky hemlines that stop dangerously high in the front and back, but drapes a little lower on the sides. My mother always likes to say that the hemline looks like a damn mullet. Party in the front and business in the back, or in this case the sides.

To finish out the look, I grab some of my chunky gold bangles and a strappy pair of gold heels. My hair hangs loose and in messy waves, giving it an 'I don't care; I'm fucking fabulous' style. I decide to keep my make-up natural and accent my blue eyes with some gold coloring.

I have to admit I look hot. If I were a dude, I would be all over this. Smiling to myself, I grab one of my smaller clutch bags and head off to Izzy's, still thinking about what will happen if Greg Cage steps into my path again.

We leave Izzy's late because all the girls are too busy loving on Nate. I might not have the tugging urge to become a mother, but even I can admit how perfect Izzy's little family seems.

Axel has hired a limo to drive us around tonight, and I am thankful not to have to drive my old '96 Honda tonight. It really is only a matter of days before the damn thing blows up.

I've met Dee and Emmy a few times before now, I don't know Emmy as well as I know Dee and Izzy, but when that girl gets some alcohol in her, she is hilarious. We end up grabbing a quick dinner before heading off to Club Carnal where we will be spending the majority of our evening.

"Whatever you do, do not get her started on the crazy drinks." Dee warns me for the millionth time. Izzy gives her another eye roll before signaling the bartender for another round.

"What will it be ladies?" He says with a wink. He eyes Izzy's rock before moving his eyes on to the rest of us. Looks like someone is on the prowl, which is perfect for this horny little bitch.

Pushing Dee out of the way, I lean over the side of the bar, bringing my lips right up to his ear. "How about you give me a Royal Fuck?" Pulling back, I have the benefit of watching his eyes flare with lust. He isn't anything to write home about, but at least he stands taller than I do with my heels on. Not many men do. His face is… pleasant. I don't get the head to toe hot flashes I get with Greg, but some tingles are better than nothing.

His eyes, even in the dim light of the club, show his heated desire. "Royal Fuck, hmm? How about you wait a few hours and I can give you a good old Southern Screw." His eyes zoom in on my cleavage, and he licks his lips. Typical man.

"Just give me something good. I'm easy to please." I run my tongue over my lip, give him another wink and turn to talk to a slack-jawed Dee.

"What?" I ask.

"Holy shit, I think even I got turned on by that." She giggles and looks down at my chest. "You're so about to lose a nipple soon."

I look down to make sure the girls are behaving and sure enough, one of those sneaky little bitches is about to join the party. Situating the funbags, I turn and smile at Izzy, who is once again looking at her phone.

"Why don't you just tell him to come here? You might as well, since you can't keep your hands off your phone." I give her a warm smile. Jealousy is a new thing for me. I never thought I would be envious of someone in a relationship. Melissa Larson doesn't *do* relationships. But, seeing how in love my friend is, and watching that love returned to her… well, for once, I have some doubts about singledom.

"He said he might stop by later, but the boys won't let him leave without at least one lap dance." She laughs, clearly finding this funny.

"Okkkkay, so for now why don't you put that damn phone away and come dance with me?"

"YES! Come on bitch, let's dance!" Dee grabs her hand, nodding her head in Emmy's direction before pulling Izzy onto the crowded dance floor.

"Come on Emmy, let's go make some wet dreams come to life tonight." She tries to pull away, but I grab her and join the girls on the floor.

I have always loved to dance, to just let the music sweep me away. It doesn't take long before sweat is covering my skin, and my mind is blissfully blank.

CHAPTER 4
Melissa

With Will.I.Am and Brittany Spears' 'Scream & Shout' blasting through the club, I smile up at the stranger in front of me, roll my hips, and rub my hands down the side of my body. God, it feels so good to let go and enjoy the moment. Meeting the stranger's eyes again, I am momentarily confused when I see a flash of disappointment before he turns his back and walks away.

"Ah, so we meet again." Even though the music is pounding into my body, consuming my soul, his voice sounds like pure fucking silk against my ear. His heavy hands grasp my hips, pinching slightly when he digs them in deep. Before I have time to react, his body molds to my back, his heat making my already feverish skin catch fire. I'm not a small woman, but this man makes me feel as though I am. The soft fabric of his pants rubs against my naked legs as we move together with the music. How fitting that the song just changed to the pulsing beats of 'Turn Me On' by David Guetta & Nicki Minaj. I have no idea who this man is, but I instantly feel the pull, the pull to turn around and jump on him. I have never felt an attraction so strong. Well, at least I hadn't until yesterday at work.

And that is the last thought I have before the strong hands spin me around, and I come face to face with Cage.

Uncle Greg Cage. Well, these are certainly not familial feelings running through my veins right now. I bring my arms up to his strong biceps and hold on tight. One of his powerful thighs pushes through my legs and just like that, I feel like a bitch in heat.

"What's your name, beauty?" he whispers into my ear. His hands move from my hips to my thighs, brushing his fingers against the swell of ass. I feel the draft hitting my naked skin, and if he pulls my dress up any further, the club will get one hell of a show. It might be crazy or just a testament to how badly I need some action, but despite meeting this man just yesterday, it feels right. Regardless of the fact that we are in a public place, my body wants this and my mind is catching up. His fingertips caress my skin, making slow, deliberate sweeps. My body presses tightly to his, and the heat from his chest makes my erect nipples burn. "Mmm, fuck... you feel like fucking heaven." His blue eyes are burning into my own, begging for permission to drag me away from here.

I look around for the girls, and after a few sweeps of the club, find them at the bar, openly gawking at the spectacle we must be making. Dee is laughing so hard it looks as though she might fall off the stool. The dark haired man behind her is too busy shooting daggers into her back to pay us any attention. A blonde God next to him is laughing just as hard as Dee. *What in the hell is so funny?* Emmy is sitting silently as usual, but her attention isn't on me and Greg. No, her attention is on the tall, broody man next to her. My eyes meet Izzy's, and I can tell she is holding it back, but wants to laugh just as hard as everyone else. And with thick arms around her shoulders, pulling her tight against his body is, you guessed it, a laughing Axel.

All of these people have lost their damn minds.

Greg brings me back to him as I feel his fingers move closer to my center. My center that I'm sure is doing a bang up job at leaving a wet spot on his leg. I might play a good game, but this man is making my resistance crumble. I am a fool to think I can ignore this chemistry.

Bringing my hands up to his chest, I push off slightly. My body ignores my mind's request to disengage contact with this fine as hell man. "Cage, Uncle Greg, was it?" I ask, pulling every little bit of my inner snark out.

His laughter rumbles up and vibrates my fingertips, causing me to pull my hands back. He uses this opportunity to crush my body into his. I have no choice but to wrap my arms around his neck when he bends down and brings his lips back to my ear. He is still rolling his hips with mine to the beat of the music, and when his erection presses firmly into my belly, I can't help the half gasp, half moan that crawls up my throat. He answers with a growl of his own and squeezes my ass between his large hands. "Your body wants this as bad as your mind does. I can feel how wet you are. Come on beauty, let's get out of here." His lips crawl slowly down my neck, and I feel his teeth clamp down lightly before he sucks lightly.

Is this motherfucker sucking my skin?

I'm about to offer him one hell of a slap in the face when I feel his hand slip around the front of my body, back under my skirt, and his fingertips brush against my screaming core. Shocks zap from my clit to my toes, arms, and head, making me feel like I might fall to the floor.

"Do you taste as good as you feel? Warm and juicy? Like a ripe peach that's mine for the picking?" He rumbles in my ear, swirling his thumb against my swollen bud. As loud as my mind is screaming to push him away, my body is screaming even louder to hold the hell on and let him take me right here in the middle of the club.

He brings his hand up, and before I can even blink, he has his thumb in between his lips, sucking my arousal off his finger.

Holy fuck.

He brings his face close to mine, until his lips are just a breath away. "Ripe enough to fucking devour." And then, he crushes his lips to mine. My gasp works in his favor, and his tongue moves in, caressing and rolling with mine.

Minutes. Seconds. Hours. I have no clue. This man has shorted every cell in my brain. Shut it all down. I am working on complete autopilot, but enjoying every fucking second of it. Until I hear a shrill voice shriek in my ear.

"Who the fuck is this bitch?" Err, what? It takes my mind a second to register what the fuck that bitch just screamed. Detangling my hands from Greg's messy brown locks, I turn on wobbly legs and face the person behind the annoying screech.

"What the hell did you just call me?" Seething is a good word to describe the way I am feeling in this exact moment. Greg has effectively wound me tight, and then forgot to press release. Lucky or unlucky, depends on which side of the coin you're on. This bitch is going to be the perfect person to help with that.

"Does *that* belong to you?" I ask Greg. He looks pissed, but not ashamed. Interesting. "Excuse me, Greg. Is this shit yours?" I ask again, pointing my finger at the malnourished bimbo in front of me.

"No," He finally says, trying to pull me back towards him by my hips, "She definitely does not belong to me."

I turn my head around and lock eyes with him long enough to give anorexic Barbie the upper hand. I feel her claws take hold of my hair and pull, ripping me from Greg's hold. "Get your skank ass away from my man," she yells, jerking me back. I feel Greg's fingers dig in painfully before he loses his grasp. Oh, but not because of this little shit. No, he loses his grasp because I twist my body from his hold and turn on her. I probably lose a few hundred pieces of hair in the process, but it's so worth it to see her face.

"Do not put your nasty little hands on me. Ever. I will make you sorry you even stepped into my mother fucking personal space! Do you hear ME, Skipper?" I get up in her face and have the pleasure of looking down into her shocked brown eyes. One thing I love about being so tall, no one will ever look down on me. "You do not want to piss me off. You think he's yours? By all means take him, but something tells me *he* doesn't want *you.*"

"You little bitch!" She screams and reaches out to slap me. This chick must have a death wish. Waiting for the last second, I reach up, grab her slim wrist, and squeeze, applying enough pressure that I know she will have marks. I offer her a sweet smile and a wink right before I take my foot and sweep her legs out from under her, watching her flailing arms and legs crash right onto the dirty floor.

I crouch down and get my face nose-to-nose with hers. "You do not look at me. You do not talk to me. You definitely do not touch me. Now, get your ass off the floor. You look ridiculous."

She takes her time climbing back to her feet, and the whole time, her eyes never leave mine. This bitch is trouble, more trouble than I care to deal with, and something tells me there is a connection between these two. I don't give a shit how hot the sex could be; I want nothing to do with this complication.

"Run along now." I shoo her away with my hands before turning around and locking eyes with the shocked face of Greg Cage. This time I have the added benefit of knowing all his friends have seen it all. Dammit. I know better than to let my temper out.

"Holy shit… that was so fucking hot, beauty!" He goes to pull me to him again, but I step out of his reach.

Stay strong, Meli. Do not let him suck you in.

"Not happening. I might have let you jumble up my head once, shame on me… but it won't happen again big boy. You have some issues with your little bitch, and those are issues I want nothing to do with." I pat his cheek once before walking over to Izzy, who is no longer able to hold in her laughter.

"Oh my God! Meli, that was the funniest shit I have ever seen in my life! You're like some secret little badass under all that sexy, aren't you?"

"Very funny! Look, I'm going to get out of here. Call you in the morning?"

"Sure thing babe! See you Saturday morning!"

I say a quick goodbye to everyone before walking out into the warm summer air. I make quick work of catching a cab, and take my ass home. Home, where I can't get into any more trouble for the night.

CHAPTER 5
Greg

What the fuck is that? When Axel pitches a fit that a toddler would be proud of in the middle of the strip club, we know the party is over. The second the stripper walks in front of him, he all but knocks the table over to get away. Goddamn pussy. Piling into a few taxis, we head over to Carnal to meet the girls. My jaw hits the floor and my dick hits the roof when I see Nurse Fuck Me on the dance floor. Fuck me, the way she is moving…

Like a homing device, my dick follows her movements, and before I know it, I am being lead right to her. Her skin is shining under the lights; her hips are begging me to take her and take her hard. She has no idea I am standing right behind her, but the douchebag in front of her sure the hell does. All it takes is one hard-as-nail look and a shake of my head, and he is running like a little bitch.

Just the memory of the way her body felt against mine has me ready to explode. Her taste is still heavy on my tongue and the pressure in my balls is enough to make me desperate.

Closing my eyes and taking a few steady breaths, I turn and get ready to head back over to the bar. Sure as shit, I must look like an idiot standing, unmoving, in the sea of gyrating bodies, with a noticeable erection. Might as well have a sign attached to my body saying I am a dirty fucking pervert. I turn around and almost knock someone to the ground in my impatience and frustration.

Mandy.

Of course, it's fucking Mandy. I'm beginning to wonder if this bitch is stalking me, always turning up.

"What the fuck was that?" I sneer at her.

She doesn't even attempt to hide the jealousy, and pissed off vibes roll off her.

"I should be asking you the same thing! Who the hell was that bitch?" And here I thought I looked stupid standing in the middle of the club with a raging hard on. No, now I have to look like an even bigger tool with Mandy pulling her shit again.

"How many times do I have to explain to you, Mandy? You have no say in what or who I spend my time with. You and me? No. Just no." I can tell that is the wrong thing to say when her face gets all contorted and bright red. "Jesus Christ. Not here." I mumble.

Walking off, knowing damn well she is going to follow me, I pass my idiot friends doing their best imitation of fucking hyenas and set off for Jeremy.

Shortly after opening up a few years back, Jeremy had run into some trouble with the wrong people. In debt over his eyeballs and starting to sink fast, he didn't hesitate to ask for help. I had known Jeremy going on thirty years, since we were two little snot nosed shits tormenting other kids in our kindergarten class. He needed help, so I stepped in. Very few people know I am the majority owner of Club Carnal. Hell, even after all this time, Izzy and Dee are in the dark. I do what needs to be done to keep my friends safe and that's it.

I catch Axel's hard look across the floor and shake my head letting him know it's all good. Walking down the dark hallway in the back, I can hear Mandy's fuck-me shoes clicking quickly behind me.

I don't even give her a second to catch up before I climb the back steps to the office two at a time.

"Greg," she whines, "I can't keep up!"

"I don't fucking care." And I don't. I would much rather chase that goddess out the front door than deal with more of Mandy's jealous bullshit. Time and time again, I have explained to her that we will never be more than a way to scratch an itch.

I knock a few heavy beats on the office door and step back to wait for Jer to unlock. Mandy finally makes it up the stairs and huffs a few times, crossing her arms and throwing me one pissed off look. I might not like the chick outside of my bedroom, but I would be blind to miss how her tits are about to spill out of her dress.

Fuck. My dick throbs in my pants again, reminding me how close to blowing I am. Reaching out to knock again, I almost slam my fist into Jeremy's face.

"What?" He asks. One thing about Jeremy, he's a 'roll with the flow' kind of guy, but he hates to be dragged into drama.

"Need the office." One look into my eyes has got to tell the story. I seem trapped between fury and lust. It's hard to tell which will win out.

"Yeah, yeah… clean your shit up when you finish." He eyes Mandy a few times before backing down the hallway and disappearing down the stairs. Fuck.

"Get your ass in there, Mandy." Holding the door wide, I follow her strut into the office and lock the door behind me. Why do I always end up in this goddamn office?

"Well? Want to tell me what the fuck that was down there?" Walking over to the desk, I lean my ass against the wood and cross my arms.

"Come on, Greg! How can you expect me to sit back and watch you basically fuck that bitch out there? Not even a few days ago, it was me you were fucking!"

"Damn woman, do you ever *not* screech?"

"You are mine Greg Cage, and I don't like seeing you touching another woman." She complains, trying to get some tears past the Botox in her face.

The song 'Crazy Bitch' seems to be playing on a constant loop these days when Mandy is around.

"I sure as hell am not. You knew, and you have always known what this is. Sex, Mandy. I want to get my dick wet, then maybe I'll call. I don't need you throwing your shit around my feet. I want to get my dick wet somewhere else, that isn't your fucking say either."

Her eyes flash and she forgets her 'sadness' for a second. Long enough for me to see the fake bitch behind all that painted on sex.

"Goddammit!" I roar and shove off the desk, walking right into her space, "You do not get to come into my life and act like I am your property. Swear to Christ, I will drop your ass quicker than you can say fuck me harder!"

"But Greg…" I don't even give her a second to speak before I take her by the shoulders and bring her body close to mine. No way is she getting this shit twisted.

"You want my dick bad enough? You want my dick, knowing I won't be thinking about you when I take you?" I ask, pulling her even closer. "Is that what you want, Mandy? Because I sure as fuck can give you what you want, but there will be no question that when I empty my balls into your body that you will not be the one I wish is taking it."

She whimpers a few times but I can tell she's made her decision. This bitch doesn't want me; she wants what I can do to her body.

She doesn't waste any time dropping to her knees and unzipping my pants. I groan when I feel her warm hand brush across my dick. Closing my eyes, I picture the blazing blue eyes of my unknown beauty.

Mandy pulls my pants down, and my dick sings hallelujah to the heavens, springing loose, and almost taking her eye out in his impatience. Goddamn, when was the last time I was this hard? I open my eyes and look down at her. Her blonde hair is all wrong, her eyes aren't blue, and her body doesn't scream fuck me. My dick doesn't know the difference though; he can feel the heat of her lips seconds before her tongue darts out and gives a long lick from root to tip. She takes her time, rimming the hoop and licking the drop of come about to fall to the floor. When she wraps her lips around me and sucks deep, I know this won't last long.

Pumping my hips into her mouth and listening to her gag on my length brings me back to earth. Her hand wraps as far around my thickness as she can get it, and even trying her hardest, she is probably only getting a few inches into her mouth. What a waste.

"Get up." I order. She is quick to pull herself from the floor. Her cheeks are flush and her dress has fallen, exposing one tit already.

I lead her over to the couch, and all but throw her down. She looks up at me, letting her legs fall open and exposing her naked flesh to my eyes. She might be a pain in my ass, but fuck if that pussy doesn't beg me to take it. I can see her wetness leaking out onto the couch.

"Does it turn you on to throw your shit around me? Trying to mark what isn't yours to fucking mark?" I ask, slowly unbuttoning my shirt. "Does it make you wet to think about my dick inside someone else's body? Hmmm?" Shrugging off my shirt and walking to stand before her, I let her take in every single inch of my body. "You remember *this*," I stress, grabbing my cock in my hands and giving a few slow and measured pulls with my fist. "This is never going to be yours." I bend over and snag a condom from my wallet, standing to my full height and rolling it on slowly, never once breaking eye contact with her.

Reaching down, I drag her hips to the edge. She lets out a shocked squeak that quickly turns into a moan when I push into her in one quick thrust. I take myself so deep I can feel myself bottom out.

"*Fuck,*" I hiss.

"Oh, Greg, baby! I love your cock!" She screams, reaching up and grabbing her tits. Even I can't ignore how fucking hot that is. "Harder, baby. Fuck me harder!"

"Shut up!" I pant. My hips are moving so rapidly I can hear the legs of the couch shifting across the floor.

Closing my eyes, I replace the blonde hair and brown eyes; under my skin, I can almost feel *her*. If I keep my eyes closed, I can almost pretend it's *her* that I am pounding into. "Beauty." I whisper.

I give a few more thrusts, and know I need to hurry this show up. I pull out and flip her over. Her grunts and groans sound more bestial than erotic. When I grab her hips and slam back into her, she lets out a high pitch scream that earns a hard smack on her ass. "Shut the hell up, Mandy; you aren't fucking trying out for a porn."

She snaps her head around and tries to shoot me with a hard look, but when I slam back into her, her eyes roll, she throws her head back, and screams out her release. The walls of her pussy clamp down hard... or at least try to; it would help if she weren't so used.

Skin slapping, moans, grunting, and a good sheen of sweat-filled minutes have me grabbing her hips and pushing in hard. When my come shoots into the condom, the only thing I can think of is how much I regret taking Mandy again.

Even nameless, my nurse has ruined me.

I pull out, slide the condom off, and walk over to the private bathroom to clean myself off. Suddenly, the only thing on my mind is showering her shit off my body.

"Greg, baby?" I hear her voice coming from the other room.

"Not your baby, Mandy."

"You can't seriously say you didn't feel anything just then? I know you felt it; you can't hide your reaction to my body!"

Is she for real?

"You want to know what I felt? I really don't know how to be more honest with you. You know there will never be anything more here, so give the hell up. What I felt was a serious case of blue balls forming if I didn't take care of the situation that another woman had me in. Not you, Mandy. You got the after effects of another woman leaving before I could finish."

"You fucking asshole!"

"Yeah, but then again, you knew that too."

We finish dressing in silence and right before I turn to leave, I pull her to me, making sure there is no room for miscommunication here.

"Don't cross me again. I want to play again, maybe I will call, but do not fucking cross me." I open the door and wave my hand for her to proceed me. Locking up and jogging back down the stairs, I leave Mandy to fend for herself. She got what she wanted; I got what I needed. End of story.

Everyone seems to have carried on without me, and by the time I make it back to their post at the bar, the girls have started another round of ridiculous as fuck drink ordering. Maddox and Beck seem to be the only motherfuckers as sour as I am.

"GREG!" Izzy screams. She giggles a few times and almost falls to the floor before Axel grabs her. "Gregory Cage! Why did you run my friend off? Huh? She was finally having a good time." She pouts and has some kind of silent conversation with herself for a few seconds, and then, before I can even open my mouth, she moves her attention back over to Emmy.

"Just ignore her man; she's been all over the fucking place since Dee started with those fucking pussy drinks." I look over at Beck, wondering why the fuck he is putting up with this shit again from Dee.

"Warned them last time, when the pussy drinks start coming out, I'm gone. You're on your own, motherfucker." I laugh and make quick work of saying goodbye. There's no telling how long they will stick around tonight, and after all my shit, I'm not in the mood to stick this one out.

I catch Mandy standing in the corner shooting daggers at me on my way out. It might be time to cut that one loose before she becomes even more of an issue.

CHAPTER 6

greg

The morning of Axel and Izzy's wedding is a mess. Everything seems to be going wrong. Axel is having a fit trying to keep Izzy calm over the phone. Dee won't stop blowing my phone up about every fucking thing from flowers to condoms for Axel. Last time I checked, he is a grown fucking man and can take care of that shit on his own. The last call about grabbing Izzy's panties before leaving their house is met with the dial tone. I might love her like a sister, but no fucking way I am digging through her underwear.

I have managed to get all the small fires out before finally making my way back to their house. Emmy has been frantically setting up the backyard for the reception to follow the wedding. After spending all day yesterday setting up the tents and tables, not much is left to do other than the chairs and shit. Between the two of us, we manage to finish it up and make it back to the church in time to get ready.

Before I can even throw the truck in park, she climbs out and runs. Not just runs, but takes off in some mad sprint like someone just yelled cake at fat camp.

"Emmy!" I yell across the parking lot. "Babe, what's the hurry?"

"Don't give me your sass, Greg Cage! You know we were supposed to be here an hour ago."

I call bullshit. Emmy might be many things, but she is shit at hiding something that's weighing hard on her.

"Try ten minutes ago, babe. What's really got you tied up? You've been quiet this week."

She quirks her brow at my quiet remark. Truth is, she is always quiet and always assessing. Axel is convinced she has some magical powers. Izzy thinks she is trying to make herself invisible. I think she just has a bad crush on the wrong dude.

I know what's eating her today. Maddox is bringing a date. No one we know, but he told Izzy the other day to expect one. I think his exact words were, "Girl, gotta date." Luckily, Iz speaks Maddox Locke, because even now, after almost fifteen years, I still don't understand the motherfucker. This wouldn't have been a big deal, but he waited until Iz was chatting with Emmy up front at the office to make his grand announcement. Subtle.

"Em." I say, "Don't waste your time. As much as I hate to say it, Locke is just never going to be the man you wish he was." She closes her eyes tight, nods her head, and spins on her heels. Before I can even breathe, she disappears.

I make a mental note to pull him aside and remind him again that he needed to set this straight. I'm sick of watching her mope around and wait for something that will never happen.

After grabbing my tux out of the truck, I take off into the church and search out my girl. Ever since the first day I meet Izzy, even though the circumstances sucked, I have known that she will always hold a piece of my heart, a piece I thought was forever lost when Gracie died. It isn't hard to love her. Watching her struggle to survive what her ex-husband put her through isn't easy.

The last year, give or take some time, has been a real struggle. In a sense, I am beyond relieved that someone I consider blood isn't in danger; won't *be* in danger. But, the flip side of that is the knowledge that she doesn't *need* me anymore. Sure, she will always need me, but not the same way. She doesn't need me to make sure her demons will stay away. I don't think I will ever get used to the fact that my girl doesn't need my protection anymore.

I can even admit to myself that I have a hard time trusting even Axel with her. It just hits too close to the pain. *Grace.* There isn't much about Izzy that doesn't remind me of Gracie. The only difference is that Gracie... Gracie didn't win. She didn't win, and I wasn't there to make sure she did. Walking Izzy down the aisle today will be bittersweet. Beyond bittersweet. My girl found her other half, finally, and they deserve this. But even knowing this, I can't help the crushing wave of pure agony that swims through my body.

My Gracie will never know this happiness. My Gracie isn't here because I couldn't keep her safe.

Never again, I vow. I will never let anyone or anything stand between those I love and their happiness.

"This church is too damn big," I curse, walking the maze upon maze of hallways. Checking my watch and noting the time doesn't help my panic one bit.

"Yo! G-Man. You keep muttering to yourself instead of getting your ugly mug ready, there won't be a wedding." Coop. Damn. If anyone could hold me up even longer, it will be this bastard.

"Well, then help me out asshole. Where can I go get ready?"

"Hey, you think there will be some single ladies here tonight?" he asks, completely ignoring me. I can feel the sweat prickling my skin. My jaw drops and my head pounds as he goes on and on about his mission. Idiot.

A slap him on the back of his sexed up head finally gets him to shut up about how weddings are a perfect place to look for new pussy. "Don't say pussy in church, motherfucker."

"Oh yeah? Because motherfucker is better?"

"Zeke Cooper... so fucking help me, tell me where the hell to go get into the monkey suit."

He opens his mouth to answer, but is cut off by Izzy's sweet voice calling down the hall, "G! Get in here!" She must have been standing there long enough to listen to

Coop's one-sided conversation about how pussy at weddings is the best, because they are all desperate for some good dick.

"Don't fuck this day up by trying to get your dick wet." I can hear his laughter trailing behind me as I take off in a jog towards where I heard Izzy's voice.

I can hear the female chatter before I even make it to the door. How the hell did I miss this room on my thirty-minute search? When I open the door, what I see almost brings me to my knees. If I ever questioned the bond between Izzy and me, I have no doubts now. Pride. The overwhelming pride that takes over my system is so powerful. I haven't felt like this since Gracie called to tell me she got her first teaching job. She had been so excited to start work at the local private school, so eager to start her life.

I shake off the pain and walk over to Izzy, wrapping her up in a hug that must have been a little too tight.

"Get off her, you overgrown ape!" She giggles against my shirt at Dee's scorn. "You mess up her makeup, and I will kick your ass."

"Shut up, Dee." I pull back and smile down at Iz. "You look beautiful, baby girl."

Her eyes immediately start to fill with tears, and I look around, trying to figure out a way to fix whatever the fuck I just broke. When my eyes land on the one person I didn't expect to see, my body fills with instant heat. *Fuck!* I step back from Izzy so she doesn't feel what this beauty has done to my body with just a glance.

I cough a few times and bring my attention back to my girl. "You ready?"

"Yes!" She all but screams in my face.

"Move, dumbass." Dee grumbles next to me.

"What the hell is wrong with you?"

"Nothing."

"Yeah, nothing my ass. Let me guess, you and Beck are playing hide and seek again? One of these days, you two will learn that it's more fun to play hide and hump."

"You are such... such... Jesus, that sounds like something Coop would say."

I laugh because really, that is something that would come out of his mouth.

"Maybe so, but damn... when the hell are you two going to get your shit together?"

She gives me a cold look before turning back to Izzy and doing whatever the fuck chicks do to make something already perfect the same.

"Go get ready." She bites out.

I turn around looking for the bathroom, and lock eyes with Nurse Sex. Fuck me, she is beautiful. Pure lust unlike anything I have ever felt hits me. I know the connection is powerful between us but this is beyond even that. Her eyes take in my appearance; all faded jeans and old black tee glory. Her eyes meet mine briefly before taking a slow ride down my body. On her way back up, her eyes pause on my dick. There is no way she can miss how turned on I am. She licks her lips before meeting my eyes and with a quirk of her lips, a wink, and a throaty laugh, she turns on her heels and walks back over to Izzy and Dee.

With my back still turned to the females clamoring about this and that, I quickly place my hand over my rock hard dick and squeeze, mentally reminding myself to play nice today. This is about Izzy and Axel, not my hormones.

Turning slowly and making sure my dick is under control, I walk over to where my bag is and take one more look at beauty. Skintight red fabric hugs her body, her tits are covered, but that doesn't do anything to hide their perfection. Right when I'm about to turn around, I notice the shoes. Tall as fucking hell and leopard print. Her tanned legs look a mile long, and immediately, visions filter through my mind of them wrapped tight around my thrusting hips, with those shoes digging into my ass. So much for having my shit in check. Groaning slightly, I grab my bag and stomp over to the changing room in the corner.

It's going to be a long fucking day.

CHAPTER 7
Melissa

Well, that was interesting. Laughing to myself, I move my eyes from the door that just slammed, back to the girls, the girls that are looking at me with calculating eyes.

"What?" I innocently ask. These girls might not have known me long, but it doesn't take much for another woman to recognize the feeling of off the charts sexual desire.

"Don't give me that crap, Meli! You two were practically having sex in the middle of the room. I know eye fucking when I see it." Izzy starts laughing at Dee's outburst. I can't tell if she's pissed or just being a bitch.

"Uh... is there something going on between you two? I didn't mean—"

"Hell no!"

"Okaaay. Then the problem is what?" I meet Izzy's eyes, and she seems to find great humor in this. Well, at least she's calmed down some. You would think she was expecting the world to fall apart around her if she doesn't get married as soon as possible.

"No problem." Dee mumbles and walks out the door.

"Don't worry about her; she just needs to cool off. Some drama between her and Beck, but believe me, you will get used to it."

Emmy walks back in a few minutes later with a bright smile and hands Izzy a blue box.

"What's this?" She questions.

"What do you think?" She replies with a smile.

"He got his?"

"Oh yeah. I left to a bunch of overgrown idiots making fun of him for choking up over some cufflinks." I meet Emmy's laughing eyes and let out a few giggles of my own. *Giggling. Really Melissa?* The more I hang out with the girls, the more I'm starting to feel like a walking billboard for cheer.

I can understand the guys thinking it's funny, but when Izzy explains the meaning behind the angel wing cufflinks that she found for her future husband, even I get a little misty.

We watch as she flips the lid and brings out a single chain. She gasps softly and sinks down to the chair behind her, just rubbing her thumb over whatever is attached to the bottom.

"What the hell happened in the two minutes I was in the bathroom?" The deep rumble comes right behind me, causing me to jump slightly.

"Nothing, G. Shit, calm your ass." I haven't heard Emmy get such an authoritative tone before. Damn, if I was into chicks that would be kind of hot.

"What is it, Baby Girl?" He asks, kneeling down in front of her. This is the first glance I have of him in his wedding garb. Holy shit, he can clean up nice. His dress shirt looks made for his body and his alone, pulled tight across his muscular frame. The way he is bent over gives me a perfect view of his tight ass. His brown hair is gelled and styled to calm the unruly locks. He looks all man and pure sex.

And I thought it was going to be easy to resist this man.

I give him a few more sweeps of my hungry eyes before moving my attention back to whatever Axel has sent over to Izzy.

"Isn't it perfect?" She whispers to Greg.

"Yeah," he whispers back. They say a few more things, softly and clearly meant only for their ears, before she throws her arms around his neck and holds tight. Dangling from the chain in her hand is a wing shaped locket. She must have opened it to show Greg what was inside because staring back at me is an inscription on one side and on the other, a picture of their adorable son. Whatever it says clearly holds some powerful meaning to them.

"What's it say?" I quietly ask Emmy.

She sniffles a few times before answering, "It's Latin for 'Love Conquers All'."

After that, it takes a few minutes to calm Izzy down and fix her makeup. Greg is clearly unhappy about her being upset again. Their connection is so strong you can almost feel it. The jealousy that I feel towards that is not something that I'm used to or something I like.

At 5:00, we make our way back up to the top floor of the church, and I give Izzy a tight hug before Emmy and I find our way down to our seats. I take one look at Axel, standing in the front with a big smile on his face, before settling in next to the rest of the boys from his security business.

Axel and Izzy have decided to keep the wedding party small, and by small, I mean one person each. Izzy's is Dee, and after Greg walks her down the aisle, he will take his place next to Axel.

Now, where their wedding party is small, their guest list isn't. Izzy explained to me that since moving his company from California, and joining up with Greg, their security and investigation business has become the go to company in Atlanta. They invited what looked to be the whole population of Atlanta.

When the music starts and Dee makes her way down the aisle, it reminds me of the last wedding I attended. The last wedding I was the Maid of Honor for. But just looking at these two, I know this marriage will have a much longer lifespan.

When everyone is busy staring at the bride, I am busy looking at her walking partner. I am really beginning to doubt my quest to stay away from him. When his eyes meet mine through the crowded sanctuary, I know it was only a matter of time before we collide.

The ceremony was beautiful. Even with my jaded heart, I can admit that much. There is no doubt in my mind that Izzy has lucked out and found one of the good ones. I know little about her past with her ex-husband, but what I do know makes me happy my friend has found this. And because of that, even I was wiping tears away by the time they said 'I do'.

They keep the ceremony short and sweet, asking everyone to please join them for the reception to follow. When they reach the end of the aisle, Axel pulls her into his arms and crushes his lips to hers. When his fist thrusts into the air as a symbol of victory, and he pulls back to look into his wife's eyes, Emmy reaches down and grabs my hand. She is a mess, crying and vibrating with extra hormones. I want nothing to do with that, but the lump in my throat is having fun calling me a liar. There is just no way to watch a love like that unite and not feel it.

I sit with Emmy, and talk about the reception to follow for at least ten minutes or so. We are waiting for the congestion in the parking lot to clear out before we head over to the reception. At the same time, I also try to avoid the look of contempt coming from the corner of the church lobby. I can literally feel the eyes on me this very second. Talk about creepy.

When a shadow falls over me, I am ready to turn around snapping, but when I look up and meet Greg's blue eyes, I quickly snap my mouth shut. His already handsome face is taken over by a look that is pure peace and happiness. I can already feel the tingles of arousal coiling in my gut.

"Beauty, you need a ride?" He asks me, interrupting my inner slut. His eyes darken slightly, and there is no mistaking the real question behind those words.

"Depends on what kind of ride we're talking about, stud."

He laughs, and even that sounds like sex. "If I thought you were serious, I would tell you to jump on, babe."

"You two really should just go lock yourselves in the confessional and get it over with." Emmy interrupts.

I look over at her, begging her to shut the fuck up, before answering Greg's question, "Well, *babe*, I don't know what kind of ride you're offering, but it looks like that position is already filled."

"What?" I have to give him some credit. This man can play the game. He genuinely looks confused, clearly caught off guard by my reply.

"Your little friend from the other night?" I say, pointing over his shoulder to the little hooch in the corner. The look of shock on his face is almost comical. He really had no clue that she was standing there.

"Motherfucker," he grumbles under his breath. "She is not with me. Come on, Beauty, run away with me."

I look into his eyes a few seconds. I'm trying to decide if that really was a line or not, before bending over, and laughing so hard that the people left in the lobby all look over at me as if I have lost it.

"That was terrible. You want some of this, you're going to have to try harder than some cheesy ass lines."

I pick up my clutch before standing. Once again, I am reminded of how powerful and *large* this man is. In my heels, I come close to six feet tall but he still looks down on me.

"Come on, Beauty. Just a ride."

"Maybe later, stud."

"You crush me," he says dramatically, clutching his hand to his heart.

"Does that work for you on the ladies?" I ask, a smile coming over my face. It's been a while since I found myself enjoying a man's company.

"Haven't a clue. Never bothered enough to try. I'll settle for a dance later, but only if you tell me your name."

I hadn't realized until this moment that I was a complete stranger to this man.

"I don't know..." I trail off, looking down at Emmy, only to find her looking across the lobby where the other three Corps Security men stand. The lightheartedness has left her face. "Maybe later," I throw out before grabbing her hand and pulling her through the lobby.

Right before we round the corner that will take us to my car, I turn around and lock eyes with Greg. He doesn't look disappointed. No, he looks like I just handed him one hell of a challenge. One that he plans on being the victor of.

CHAPTER 8

Greg

How the hell did I strike out with her again? I've been fighting the urge to throw her over my shoulder and run since I saw her down in Izzy's dressing room. The whole time I was standing up there next to Axel, my eyes kept finding her in the crowd. Wasn't hard, that red dress was like a waving flag, and I was the raging mad bull. There was no doubt in my mind now; I wanted her and I wouldn't stop until I had her.

"You do realize that your little plaything is turning into a DEFCON 2 stalker, right?" Beck leans up against the wall beside where I stand watching Emmy and my mystery woman walk to an older model car. She turns and gives me another wicked, full of promise stare before dropping into the driver's seat.

"That's some serious shit you need to deal with, but if those tits look as good in person as they do from across the room, I'd be happy to help you out. You know, take one for the team."

"Shut the fuck up, Coop."

"Problem?" Locke asks, walking over. His date for the evening, an attractive looking redhead, stands off to the side looking clearly bored.

"Nothing I can't handle."

"Sure you can, that's why big tit Barbie keeps following you around like a sick little puppy."

"More like a deranged bitch," I mumble. "I have it under control. Either of you riding with me over to Axel's?"

"Just me and Coop."

I look over at Locke and catch his small nod confirming Beck's words.

"Got it. Going to take out the trash, then be ready to ride."

I have to remind myself a few times to control my temper. Control. I have to completely lock down every urge I have to get in her face and flip the fuck out. I don't do clingy women. Hell, I haven't done the same woman in years. When I met her, she was a means to an end, a way to keep my dick from falling off. I have told her from day one that there would never be more than the two of us spending time naked. No dating, no meeting friends, and no fucking acting like I am a piece of property.

There is no way Mandy is sane, standing there ready to take me on. No fucking way. She has the nerve to show up here at my family's wedding, uninvited, and throw her shit. Shit that she has no right throwing. It is past time to cut her the fuck loose.

"Amanda."

She tenses slightly at the hard tone I give her name. Literally, I'm spitting her name out with nothing but disgust dripping from my tone. I take her by the elbow and lead her off to the side hallway, away from listening ears.

"Would you like to tell me why in the fuck you are here?"

"Because baby, I knew you would want me to share this day with you." I have to give the bitch credit; she honestly believes this bullshit. If I didn't know better, I would think she really did want to be here. But I do know better, and I know there is nothing but calculating crazy-as-fuck scheming underneath the fake.

What. The. Fuck.

"Are you stupid? Please tell me you're just slow, and missed the fucking memo titled 'you are nothing but a warm body'? " She flinches slightly but not enough. Apparently, it's going to take a lot more than the normal brush off. This is going nowhere, shit.

"Don't be silly, Greg." She laughs slightly and reaches out to place her hand on mine, but I step back and watch her arm fall lamely back down.

"Listen to me, and listen to me real good, Amanda. I will not repeat this shit again. You and me, we are done. Completely and never going to fucking happen again done. The last time you will ever get my dick was last night. Whatever the hell you think is going on here, is not. I won't be your man, and I damn sure will never climb back into your body. Hear me... This. Is. Over."

I don't even give her a chance to respond. Turning around, I rejoin my boys before heading out of the church and off to the reception.

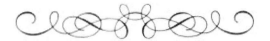

My mood isn't any better three hours later. We did the traditional bullshit that always comes with weddings: more pictures than I care to ever be a part of again, dancing, cake cutting and dinner. Now the party is going hard, and the alcohol is flowing freely.

My eyes haven't left the object of my desire since arriving. She doesn't disappoint either. It seems like she is putting on a show just for me; the only fucking problem is her using all the single men here to do so. Her favorite seems to be the one and only manwhore himself, Zeke Cooper.

I have no idea what the hell they are dancing to now; I just know he is way too fucking close. When I watch his hand slip around her waist and pull her closer, I almost break my glass. When she throws her head back and laughs, her whole face lighting up with the humor, I go over all the ways I know how to kill a man. When his palm moves to her ass and squeezes, I see red. My whole body is draws tight and the desire swirling with the rage is a hard combination to filter through.

This kind of body consuming desire is new to me. Sure, there have been plenty of women in my thirty-five years, but none that makes me feel this way. And there damn sure hasn't been one that has been able to walk away from me. Coop might annoy the shit out of me on a good day, but I have never considered ways to murder my friend before.

"You got it bad."

"You have no idea." I look over at Locke, noticing his eyes aren't watching Coop and his partner, but are looking across the room at the table Emmy is sitting at while rocking a sleeping Nate.

"Gonna do anything about it?" He finally asks, after a few minutes of silence.

"Yeah. Are you?" Clearly not expecting my question in return, he slowly turns his head and looks over at me. His dark eyes give nothing away.

"No." And with that, he walks away, rejoining his date. At least I'm not the only miserable bastard in the room.

After a few more songs, Coop takes his soon-to-be-ripped-from-his-arms hands off of her body. She looks around the room before walking over to the bar, the bar that I haven't left in almost an hour. Her eyes never leave mine. Her hips moving seductively to the music make my mouth water, and my pants tighten.

I will have her.

She walks up to the bar and asks for something. I couldn't tell you what, because when she leans over the edge, her perfect ass is on display for my hungry eyes. My mouth waters and my fingertips tingle. Just imagining my fingers digging in hard and pulling her roughly towards my straining cock causes my already strung tight body to weep.

I must have let out a groan because her head snaps up and looks me over.

"Want to take a picture?" Her question has me slowly, oh so slowly, bringing my eyes up to hers. She doesn't look pissed, which is a plus. She looks like she is enjoying this slow fucking torture.

"Dance with me." I look at her, just taking her in and wait for her to answer, a little shocked that the request even came out of my mouth. I hate dancing, but if it gets my body closer to hers, I will do anything.

"Just dance?"

"For now." Taking her hand and leaving our drinks on the bar, I lead her to the middle of the room, pulling her close and crushing her body to mine.

Having her in my arms feels like coming home. I am not one to believe in all that love at first sight bullshit, but even as cynical as I am, I can recognize something bigger than lust at work. My body wants her; that is no secret, but the level of want is borderline craving. I need her. Needing someone is not something I am used to. No, I am used to being needed... something this woman clearly doesn't want.

"What's your name, Beauty?" I ask her again. I use the rhythm of the song to rock our hips together softly. Her arms dangle over my shoulders, and if I bend over slightly, our lips will be even. My fingertips are just barely ghosting over the swell of her ass. My cock is begging me to pull her flush, to feel her body against mine.

She ignores me and smiles coyly. She might be able to play off this aloof behavior as indifference to our connection, but her eyes can't hold back. Her eyes are telling me everything I need to know. She might not have made up her mind as to what she wants but I can tell deep down she wants to find a dark room.

"Come on Beauty, tell me," I plead. I'm not past it at this point and fuck if she wants me to call her Timmy and bark like a dog, I will.

She doesn't answer, but her hands push into my hair and grab it in a firm hold, pulling the strands tightly. She comes off her heels and brings her mouth up to my ear. "What's it matter?"

Normally I would hate games, but with her, it feels like foreplay. "Babe, I need to know what to call you when I slide my dick into your body." Her gasp in my ear causes my already painfully hard dick to throb. She pulls back and looks at me; her wide blue eyes are sparkling with curiosity.

"You said just a dance." Like I need reminding.

"Didn't say we would be dancing with our clothes on." We lock eyes for a few more seconds before I hear the song change and the soulful sounds of Sam Grow's 'Lay You Down' fill my ears. If this isn't a sign, then I don't know what is. I pull her close to my body, her tits crush against my chest, and my dick pushes into her stomach. My leg pushes between hers and I begin a slow, sex-filled rhythm with our hips. Bending down so that my lips are a breath away from her ear, I softly sing the words, making sure that every single ounce of promise I possess is present in the lyrics.

Wrapping one arm around her slim waist, I trail the other slowly up her spine before cradling her head lightly, turning it slightly to give me better access.

I can feel her breath coming rapidly against my cheek, and where my thumb rests against her neck, her pulse is pounding in frantic succession.

She wants this.

We continue our slow grind to the lyrics that feel like they were made for our dance. There is no doubt in my mind that if our clothes were absent, I would be deep inside her body.

CHAPTER 9
Melissa

I might have been able to hold my reserve about staying away from this man, until he takes me in his arms and basically blows my mind with just a dance. I am willing to sign my soul over at this point. I can feel him pressing against my stomach… every rock solid inch. Each time he rotates his hips with the beat of the song, a little more wetness seeps from my body. I am primed and ready to go, all because of this man.

When the song ends, he pulls back again and looks into my eyes. "Tell me."

"Melissa," I squeak. Yes… I squeak. The games are over now; this is too raw.

"Alright, Melissa," he croons; my name curling around his tongue sends tingles across every inch of skin. "Let's start over, hmm?"

I stare at this gorgeous man and nod my head like an idiot.

"Name's Greg Cage. Most of my friends call me Greg, some call me Cage, but you can call me whatever you want."

Really? Is he for real right now?

"Does that line ever work for you? And why would I call you Cage? Sounds like something you stuff a rabid animal in." His eyes widen slightly before his rich laughter rings out around me. I'm sure I look like a crazy woman with the smile that takes over my face. Even I can tell it's a bit too happy. Good Lord, he really is good looking.

"Damn babe, you're either a lesbian or you just like chomping my balls." He shakes his head, still letting out a few soft manly laughs. "Beauty, you can call me whatever you want as long as you're screaming it."

Before I can even process his actions, he bends down and gives me a quick but deep kiss. When he pulls back and rests his forehead against mine, I know I might as well have just signed on the dotted line. The look he gives me is so full of promise that if I had been wearing underwear, they would have blown up, completely exploded, right from my skin.

"Come home with me." I blurt.

He seems to ponder that for a minute before a feral smile graces his lips. He knows he won this round. I might be giving in to the sparks flying around us, but this was just going to be sex. Nothing more.

"Tell you what, let me finish up around here, and then we can go back to my place."

"I'm not riding with you. I want my car there, just in case," I mumble the end of that, but he doesn't miss it. His eyes flash and his smile slips slightly.

Way to go Melissa, might as well take out an ad that lists all the issues you have.

"That's fine, but I can assure you that you won't want to leave for a long fucking while."

"Just sex?" I ask. No reason to beat around the bush now.

"For now." He takes my hand in his and leads me off the dance floor and back to the bar where we left our drinks. "Here's to living," he says and holds his beer up to click with my wine glass.

Seems like an odd thing to toast to when you just agreed to go off with a complete stranger and play hide the sausage. The more I think about it though, the more it honestly makes sense. I made a promise, to my sister that I would never stop living. Of course, she didn't know about this promise, but the day I made that promise to her, whispering the words to the cold earth, I felt a weight lift off my shoulders.

Well sister dear, if this isn't living, then I don't know what is.

"To living," I echo back with a smile before taking a sip.

It has been an hour since I essentially agreed to a night of unlimited possibilities. I see Greg floating around the room, stopping to spend time with the bride as well as the rest of the men in their immediate group. He seems to be aware of my every movement. I move to speak with another person, and his eyes are always burning into my skin. When my eyes meet his, it is pure fire. I could feel his gaze caressing every inch of my skin and it was slowly, agonizingly driving me out of my mind.

I want him.

"I know that look." Dee says, coming to rest at the table that Emmy and I have been sitting at for the last few minutes.

"I don't know what you're talking about."

"My ass you don't," she laughs. "That look you keep sending G is hot enough to make me start panting."

"Oh, really? You wouldn't happen to know anything about heated looks across the room, would you?" Emmy cuts in. Her tone actually shocks me. In all the times I have been around her, she has been nothing but sweet and quiet.

"What the hell, Em?" What the hell indeed.

"Look, Dee, you know I love you, but please take my advice, Beck wants you, and you keep playing games. What are you going to do one day when you change YOUR mind and want what he has been offering for almost two years and he isn't offering it anymore?"

"It's not that easy, Em." Dee rests her head against my shoulder and lets out a ragged breath, "It's just not that easy."

I look up and meet Emmy's eyes across the table, noting that her usually sweet and serine expression is hard and cold.

"It is that easy. You want him, he wants you, but you are too busy trying to push him away to give him the chance he deserves. I would love to be in your shoes. Have the man *I* want, want me back." She slams her glass down on the table, rattling all the place settings in the process. Giving her chair a shove back, she leaves the table so quickly I'm not even sure which direction she ran off in.

"Would you like to clue me in on what just happened here?" I ask Dee with a slightly manic laugh.

"That, my dear Melissa, was me being put in my place." She takes a long sip of her wine, slouching down in her seat and just dazing off into the crowd.

"Do you want to talk about it?" Izzy has filled me in some but not enough to pretend I know what is running through her head.

"Do you ever get so tired of putting on a mask, day in and day out? I'm so sick of putting on my mask." Her words are slur slightly but I think I understand what she means. God, I hate drunk people.

"Don't hide who you are, Dee. One thing I have learned is you never hide who you are. If you want something, you fight for it. When you think you have fought hard enough, fight a little more. Don't ever let anyone or any situation make who you are."

She looks over at me with wide eyes. Whatever I said must have hit the mark, but I honestly have no idea what she wants. I haven't been around them enough to tell the ins and outs, but I know there is something seriously fucked up going on between her and Beck.

"Yeah," she says with a slight wobble. "I just don't know… " she trails off when we hear a commotion across the way from where we are sitting.

Over near the edge of the property, we see what looks to be Axel carrying his bride off into the darkness. The only thing you can see is his back and a laughing Izzy over his shoulder jogging off around the house. I look over at Dee and all the sadness has left her eyes. We stare at each other for a few minutes, trying to decide if we just saw the groom kidnapping his own wife, before bursting into laughter.

We have been sitting there laughing for a few minutes when I feel him. My back prickles and my skin warms. Without looking, I know that Greg Cage is standing behind me. I feel one finger brush lightly down the side of my neck before his lips ghost against the shell of my ear, "You ready?"

I gulp, wondering for a second where the hell my strength to stay strong around this man has gone. I have to keep my walls up around someone as *dangerous* as him.

"Sir! Yes, Sir." I joke, giving Dee a wink before turning in my seat. When my eyes meet his, I see my joke might have missed the mark. His face is hard. His blue eyes look almost violet, and his hands clench tightly into fists. *What the hell?*

I stand, not wanting to be at the disadvantage…well, more of the disadvantage. At least with my shoes, we are almost equal. His breathing is coming in quick pants, his nostrils flaring. I walk as close as I can, toe-to-toe, my chest grazing his slightly, and give him a good hard look of my own.

"What is your problem?" I whisper. I can feel the heat off his lips so close to mine.

He is still giving me a good accessing look, but seems to make his mind up silently on the best way to proceed. "Say goodbye to Dee."

"Goodbye to Dee," I call over my shoulder. Her giggles reach my ears, causing me to let a few out before I school my face again. "Your turn," I whisper.

"Gone, Dee. Don't fucking drive." And with that, he grabs my hand and rushes me off through the crowd, the tent, yard, and around the house. We stop in front of the drive, standing there for a few seconds. He lets go of my hand and paces a few steps in front of me before turning around and looking at me. His breathing hasn't improved much, and a small part of me wonders if he might have asthma or some shit.

"Do you need an inhaler?" I ask.

"What the fuck?" He mumbles.

"You sound like you're about to have an asthma attack or something. So I repeat; do you need an inhaler?"

He raises one thick brow and lets out a rough laugh. "Do I need a fucking inhaler? No, I do not need an inhaler.

What I need is for you to please behave yourself in public. You can't say shit like that and not have me wanting to rip your sexy as sin dress from your body. The next time you call me Sir, it better be when you are begging for me to let you come." He reaches out and pulls my body forward, crushing his lips down against mine.

Jesus Christ. And I thought he had set my body on fire before. Hard, wet, and full of carnal heat, his tongue battles with my own for dominance. His hands fist my hair, and turn my head, and his body envelops mine.

He owns me with a single kiss.

For a single second, I have the nagging thought that I might just be in over my head with this man.

CHAPTER 10
Melissa

I followed the taillights of his truck through town and into a nice residential area. Far cry from my tiny shithole apartment. He turns his truck into the driveway and I pause for a second before pulling my piece of shit in behind him.

Well... this is embarrassing. I have never been one to let another person's wealth intimidate me, but this is slightly hard to stomach. His house is large and you can tell it's worth more than I probably can make in a lifetime. Anytime you need to drive through a guarded gate to get to your house, you know it isn't the ghetto. Now, *I* live in the ghetto.

I can hear my car clanking and sputtering as I stop next to his truck. He leans against the driver's door spinning his keys around his finger. He might look cocky to some, but to me, he looks fucking edible.

He has pulled his tie off and unbuttoned the first few buttons. His jacket is gone and he has rolled up his sleeves, revealing his strong arms. With each flick of his wrist that sends the keys spinning, you can see each and every muscle in his forearm flex. And don't even get me started on his long, nimble fingers. I have to clench my thighs together just watching them work his keys.

We stand there, with only my car standing in between us, just taking it all in. I am still trying to figure out how the hell I went from promising myself I wouldn't get tangled up with this man, to seconds away from jumping on and saying yee-haw.

"Come here, Melissa."

"No," I respond. Why I thought it was a brilliant idea to poke the bear is beyond me, but there is something thrilling about watching him walk the line of losing control.

His keys stop spinning in a second. "Babe, come here."

"Make me."

Looking back, I might be able to see how it wasn't the wisest idea of mine to try and make him snap, but I have a feeling a man like Greg Cage needs a little challenge every now and then.

"Melissa."

"Greg."

He moves so swiftly that he is nothing but a white flash in the darkness. Before I know it, his shoulder meets my belly, and I am being carried into the house. His hand against my ass sends shocks of desire up my spine. I can feel my pussy tighten with awareness, like even that bitch knows how close he is to her.

I push off his waist, trying to take in the house as he barrels up the stairs. Even with his quick and rushed movements, he is careful not to jar me on his shoulder. Deciding for some unknown reason that it would be fun to further test his control, I bring my hands from his belt, and take each of his firm cheeks and squeeze. Damn his ass is hard as a rock. His growl fills the silence that had only before held the heavy breathing of this insane man.

"Watch it, Melissa, you're playing with fire."

"Always did like it hot," I groan, bringing one of my hands up and slapping his ass. Hard. My palm tingles and sharp stabbing pain shoots up my wrist. *Fuck! I think his ass just broke my hand!*

He stops dead mid-step into what I can only assume is his room. I don't even think he is breathing. Statue still and vibrating with unleashed tension.

Uh oh.

Slowly, oh so freaking slowly, he begins dropping my feet to the floor. His face is unreadable, but he can't mask the heat in his eyes. Burning. Every inch of my skin his eyes cross over feels like it has been physically touched.

I bring my arms up and start unbuttoning his shirt. He just stands there and lets me. It takes me a second, but around button two point five, I realize his silence is nothing more than his trying to regain the control that is slipping away. No way, not having that. Grabbing both sides of his half-undone shirt, I give a hard yank, sending buttons flying around me. He lets out low rumbles deep in his throat, and his hands clench.

Running my hands from his rock hard pecs down to his abs earns me another throaty growl. When I palm his dick through his pants, his eye twitches and he sways slightly. Leaning forward, I swirl my tongue around his nipple and give a solid squeeze to his generous bulge. When I bite down on his nipple lightly, his groan turns into a fierce roar, I step back hastily, almost knocking my ass to the ground when I trip over the rug.

His hands shoot out and grab my hips to help steady my legs. "Get naked. Now," he finally pants, once he makes sure my footing is solid.

He steps back and drops his ass into a chair that I didn't even notice was there. Looking around the room, I take in the masculine warmth. All the furniture is dark wood, and cream colors the walls. Very earthy. My red dress stands out against all the muted tones. I look back over to where he is lounging and take in his arrogantly lifted brow. He doesn't think I'll do it. Stupid man.

Turning on my heel and presenting my backside to him my back, I reach up and slowly draw the zipper down the length of my back. Luckily, it isn't so high up that I need to ask for his help. I take my time, feeling the teeth unhook one at a time with the measured glide of the zipper. When it catches at the bottom, I look over my shoulder again and watch as he brings his hand to his belt.

Well, that is fucking hot.

I slip each shoulder off slowly before letting the dress drop and pool at my feet. I can't hold back my smile at the harsh intake of breath that comes from behind me. I'm certain that he didn't expect to find me completely naked beneath my dress.

I bring my leg up, but right before I slip my shoe off, I hear his strained voice say, "Leave it." I drop my foot and slowly turn to face him. I'm comfortable enough in my own skin to know I look damn good. When I complete my turn and meet his eyes, I can see that he agrees. Looking down his body, I notice that he has slipped off the shirt, and his pants are unfastened. One hand grips the arm of his chair with so much force that it looks like he might rip the arm right off, but his other hand? His other hand is slowly stroking one hell of a shock to my system.

His body alone is enough to convince me to sell my left tit just to touch it, but to see what he has been packing all day makes my center weep with wetness. Huge, thick and *decorated*. He fingers the hoop, which causes his dick to jump and a hiss to shoot from his mouth. As if the Prince Albert isn't shocking enough, the second horizontal bar through his bulbous head has my jaw dropping. My first thought was 'holy shit that had to hurt', but closely followed it is my body screaming 'hell fucking yes, that will feel like pure bliss'!

"Like what you see, Beauty?" He continues his slow strokes. I can see the drop of come that is starting to fall from the top and my mouth instantly waters. "Tell me how bad you want my dick."

Shaking my head to clear the lust-filled fog, I have to remind myself of the game I started. I don't know when it became important, but I want the upper hand. I smile sweetly. "I don't think so, big boy." I bring my hands up and caress my breasts, tracing the swell, and then cupping them and pushing them together. The friction forces a soft moan to escape. I trail one hand deliberately down my body, allowing my fingers to outline my sex a few times, and drawing the warm moisture across my soft skin. When I part my folds and drag a finger through my wetness, his hand stops stroking and his eyes flash.

"Melissa," He warns.

"*Greg,*" I moan, swirling my finger around my clit. "Tell me, how bad do *you* want my pussy?" With his answering growl, I push two fingers deep, close my eyes, and hum low in my throat. It's been a while since I had a man to pleasure my body, long enough that I know exactly what my body needs. When it became obvious that no man was able to do it for me, I forced myself to learn.

My rolling hips and moans of pleasure must be the trigger that causes him to snap. Before my eyes even finish opening, I am flat on my back and his mouth latches to my pussy. He pushes his tongue in deep and with his hands on my hips, pulls me roughly against his mouth. After a few stabs into my seeping center, he slowly licks his way up to my clit. I can see one corner of his mouth tip up, and his eyes crinkle before I feel the sharp sting of his teeth as he bites down on my swollen bud. My hands fly into the sheets, my head falls back, and with a loud scream, I come on his tongue.

"Oh my God!" I have no idea what I am screaming at him now. For all I know, I am speaking in another language. The things he is doing to my body should be illegal. Never in my life have I felt so overcome with pleasure. He continues his slow licks and nips until my body comes back down, then he trails leisurely kisses up my abdomen. He pauses briefly to lick around my belly ring before continuing his way up to my tits.

"Love these. Your tits… fuck me babe, but I could spend hours on these alone." He licks and swirls his tongue around my nipples. He makes sure to spend enough attention on each before taking my mouth with his.

His kiss is demanding and full of control. With his hands holding my head firmly between his palms, there isn't much room for me to try and regain the upper hand. Hell, at this point, I can't remember why I wanted it. The things he is doing to my body… my heart pounds as if it is seconds away from exploding and every inch of my skin feels too tight. I need him.

"Please…pl-please Greg!" I scream, wrenching my mouth from his wicked attention. My body is shaking so violently with the built up desire that I can feel my teeth knock together. "Goddammit! I need you inside my body! Fuck me!"

If he hears me, then he is clearly ignoring my begging. His lips nip at the skin around my collarbone, soothing each sting with his tongue.

To hell with this. I need his dick inside my body now. Bringing my feet up flat on the bed, I push down with all the strength I have left in my body. Clearly, I catch him off guard, making it easy to flip his large body off of my own. Using his shock to my advantage, I pounce. Before he can even move, I jump up and straddle his chest, trapping his arms under my legs. My slick pussy meets flush with the heated skin of his chest.

When he tries to speak, I cover his lips with my finger and shush him. "No." His eyes flash with warning, warning that I have every intention of ignoring. "I told you

I wanted your dick. I didn't stutter. My words, Greg, were clear. Condom?"

His tongue darts out and licks my finger, but even with the playful act, his eyes light from within. I have a feeling he is just letting me take the lead here.

"Drawer," he says with a nod towards the side table. Luckily, when I flipped him, we landed within arm's length. I lean forward, letting my breast fall heavy against his face. He doesn't waste any time before attacking. His tongue and teeth cover every inch he can reach without the use of his hands.

Grabbing a condom and then sitting back on my perch before he can try anything is harder than I think it could be. He lets out the most raw, feral sound when his lips lose purchase on my nipple.

I give him a smirk before deliberately inching my way down his body. When I get eye level with his cock, I want to cry with joy. This is going to be delicious. Ripping the condom open with every intention of making quick work of rolling it over his impressive length, I quickly realize that I have no idea how this will work. I don't know what the hell I am supposed to do with the ring and barbell. He growls, snatching the condom from my fingers before rolling it on. Right before he moves his hands, I catch another flash of metal down near his balls.

"Are you fucking kidding me?" I whisper, "Do you have some self-mutilating fetish?" Right where his shaft ends, there is a long barbell through his skin. Fuck me; it just keeps getting better and better.

"You won't be complaining about that one when it's slamming against your clit, promise you that."

"Oh God."

Climbing back up his body has me swearing that I have died and gone to hard body heaven. I lick every inch of his skin that I can reach before straddling his hips and taking his mouth. While our tongues swirl together and our breathing clashes, my hips are busy rubbing against his. My legs spread just about as wide as I can get, forcing my pussy to open like a flower and hug his dick tight.

Pushing off his chest, I lift up, grab his dick, and slam myself home. I almost can't hear the harsh bite of his breath over my scream. I feel the rings hitting a spot deep within me that will have me begging in no time. The one pressed tight against my clit has my vision going hazy.

"Have... to... move," he warns, and once again, I find myself rolled onto my back. He doesn't even pause when he flips and pounds into me. His hips slap against mine, his balls make a loud, wet sound as they hit my skin, and his eyes flash something I wish to God I understood.

"H-h-harder!"

He slams deep and leans up on his knees causing his dick to slip out almost completely. His large hands grab my hips and bring my body half off the bed. With my head still on the bed, the rest of my body hovers under his control as he pulls back and gives me my wish. My legs are dead weight, my hands clench tightly in the sheets, and my eyes hold his. The look in his eyes combined with the hard hitting of his piercings, and the awe-inspiring thrusts is enough to have me screaming. Screaming, begging, and pleading. I have lost control of my body. It is locked tight and shattering into pieces.

His hips pick up speed but then slightly slow down towards the end of my release. He brings my body back down to the mattress and rocks his hips, causing a few more aftershocks to roll through my body.

"Do you like my cock? Do you like having me so deep in your body you won't be able to walk tomorrow? The way your pussy is gripping my dick and your wetness is coating my balls, I would say you fucking love it."

I whimper and he smiles. This isn't the attractive smile he gives the public, no… this smile is pure fucking sexy evil.

"Going to fuck you raw." He warns before making true to his words. When he finally grabs my hips and locks our pelvises together, I have come twice and lost track of reality.

It takes us a good hour before we are even able to detangle our limbs. When his body crashes down on mine, he rolls slightly so I won't have issues breathing. His weight feels perfect against my body, and I can't bring myself to be alarmed at how perfect that match seems to be. Maybe it's time to let someone in.

No, even with the perfect sex I have learned enough from my sister to know it isn't wise to let a man have your heart. When that happens, it is only a matter of time before you lose yourself.

"What's got your wheels turning?" He says into my neck.

If he only knew. "Just wondering when you're going to be ready to go again."

"Fucking animal," he laughs.

CHAPTER 11

Melissa

"What does your tattoo mean?" We have just finished another rough round of the best sex I have ever had. New rule, any man I sleep with must have the trifecta of vaginal bliss. When the steel of his base piercing hits my clit, I can see angels singing in the heavens.

He is relaxed on his back with his arm slung over his head, and the tattoo I haven't noticed before is on full display. I have been running my fingers softly over the ink for a few minutes, watching his skin prickle with every stroke. I've never seen something so simple be this moving, breathtaking. There has to be at least twenty small black birds that start at his hip and fly around to his back where I assume they end around his shoulder. Intertwined in the birds are the words 'Free Yourself, Gracefully'. It can't be a coincidence the only part written in an elegant script is the word 'Grace'.

He brings his other hand over and absentmindedly runs his fingers over the last word on his ribs. "It's for my sister, Grace."

He doesn't say anything else, but continues to trace his fingers over her name.

"How long ago?" I don't need to say more; he knows what I mean.

"Almost ten years." He rolls on to his side and props his head onto his hand. "I was overseas when I got the call."

"Jesus... I'm sorry, Greg. I know that doesn't mean anything, but trust me when I say I know how you feel." I don't talk about my sister. Not even to my mother who knows exactly what I feel. I just haven't been ready. Even now, almost two years later, it still crushes me to know that she won't ever be there again.

'Beauty," he says, running one of his fingers down my face. "I have felt the pain of losing her for so long now, and not once have I met someone who could feel this. Want to give me more than that?"

"Not really... but I will," I rush to get out when I see him start to pull back. Not physically. No physically, he is very much here but his eyes lose the light. "My sister. I lost her coming up two years ago."

I flip to my stomach and move my hair out of the way. In the center of my shoulder blades is a single feather with a bird flying out from a fracture in the tip. Underneath the feather in tiny script are the words 'Take this broken wing and learn to fly'.

"Kind of weird how close our ink is." I say, trying to lighten the moment, but really, how can you make light of this shit.

"Grace would have loved you. Not many people would give me shit." His lips ghost over my ink before I feel him move away. "She was only twenty-five when she died. I didn't get the call for almost a week, a week she was gone and I had no clue that my other half…" He stops talking and visibly composes himself. "I felt it. People are always skeptical of the twin connection, but I *felt* it. It was almost like the string that connected us had snapped. Didn't know it at the time, being that I was in the middle of a battlefield but looking back, I felt it."

"How did she pass?"

"She was murdered." I gasp, the sound echoing around the room, but he doesn't even look at me. He is clearly lost in the memory. "The bastard she was married to fucked with her car. The only peace I have is that she didn't suffer in the end. Married to that piece of shit for almost five years and I didn't have a fucking clue he was beating her until it was too late."

"What?" I whisper, shocked at the sound of my own voice. I sit up swiftly and just look at him, "What did you just say?"

"Fuck, I didn't mean to get heavy, babe. Really. It's been so long since I talked about her, I just lost myself for a second there."

"He hurt her?"

He sighs deeply. "Yeah, Beauty… he hurt her."

"Fia, my sister, her husband… her husband hurt her too. Only difference was I knew; I knew and I didn't do shit because she wouldn't let me!" His arms wrap around me and pull me close to his body. I know I haven't dealt well with Sofia's death. Brushing it under the rug and marching on seems to be working, and who am I to mess with what works. My strong exterior has become who I am but deep down inside, I just want to let it all out. Scream, yell, and freak the hell out that I will never see her again.

I tried, for years to get her to leave that bastard. Every time, she would just brush it off. Then she had Cohen and nothing would get her to leave. I begged, oh how I begged. "She kept saying she was okay! How is your husband beating you o-fucking-kay?"

"You never dealt with this shit." Not a question. I go from sated to fucked up in the blink of an eye. Hello! Poster child for fucked in the head, right here!

"You know what's fucked up? I begged her, I begged her, and in the end, she fucking shot the bastard. She shot him, but not before he got to her first." He goes solid under me for a few seconds but I am too far into my memories to even process what makes him tense up. "Cohen was asleep upstairs."

"Cohen?" His voice sounds off, almost strained.

"My nephew. Coolest kid in the world."

"Nephew?" I turn to look at him when his tone finally registers.

"Yeah, Cohen. What is that look for?" He looks like he swallowed something sour. I know he likes kids, so it shouldn't be an issue that I have a nephew... Jesus. Could it be possible that I misjudged this man?

He is silent for a while, just looking into my eyes. I can tell he wants to say something; the emotion behind his eyes is one I haven't seen before, almost as if he is worried but pissed at the same time.

"What is going on with you?" I finally break the silence.

He shakes his head and brings his mouth forward to meet mine. "Nothing." He offers a few small kisses against my lips before pulling back and looking into my eyes. "Nothing, just thinking. I don't know why we crossed paths, but I can't ignore the feeling that it was for a reason."

"You aren't what I expected," I tell him.

"Right back at you, babe."

When his mouth settles against mine again, I pull him close and dive in headfirst. Before, this was all about the game. Enjoy him while I can and stay away from any kind of attachment. But now, I feel like it would be impossible to walk away. He knows; this man knows how it feels to lose someone you love. In the small amount of time we have known each other I can tell he won't be like Fia's husband. No, not Greg. This man screams white knight.

When he settles his hips against mine and sinks deep, the last coherent thought that filters through my mind is that I want him to be *my* white knight. I want him to save me from me.

We finally fall asleep when the sun starts to climb. We have sweat-covered bodies and intertwined limbs. My body is deliciously sore and still craves more of what he can give me. He has taken me twice since our talk. Twice, and the sex just keeps getting better and better. This man, oh this man knows what he is doing.

I am lying between his arms and enjoying the feeling of his hard body against mine, while trying to figure out what woke me from my deep slumber. My mind is still a foggy mess from the night before and the exhaustion is hard to shake off.

"What the hell is that noise?" He mumbles into my neck, squeezing me tighter.

"I think it's your phone?" I ask and wiggle my ass against his hardening erection.

When the noise finally stops, he rolls me over and covers my body with his. "Good morning," he says with a smile.

"Good morning." He moves to kiss me but I turn my head and cover my mouth with my hand. "No way! Morning breath!" I laugh into my palm.

"I don't care." He trails his lips down my exposed neck and nips his way to my breast. How can I argue with a man that is determined? And if I'm honest with myself, I don't want to. My body has been demanding his since the last time he pulled out.

"Spend the day here. I know you are all 'Miss Independent' and shit, but stay, please." Looking into his blue eyes and his wide smile, I know it isn't possible to tell him no. All my previous misgivings have fled, and the only thing that is left is the desire to see what exactly is going to happen with *this* thing between us.

"Yeah, I'll stay… if you make it worth it."

If possible, his smile gets even larger. He throws his head back and laugh. "I think we can arrange that." He reaches over, grabs another condom from the edge of the bed, pulls up to his knees, and offers me a wink before stroking his cock a few times. His eyes never leave mine when he rolls the condom slowly down his length.

"Tell me how bad you want my dick." He commands.

His eyes are burning so bright and the wicked promise I see in them has me answering without hesitation, "I want your dick. I want your dick bad, baby."

In a flash, he is covering my body and is stretching my sex wide with his slow entry. Our mouths fuse together; his tongue dances with mine. Each time we come together, it's hard and fast, but this is something else. I could feel him, every inch of him. It feels as if we are not just physically, but also mentally marking each other. Right down to our souls.

Powerful.

I might not be ready to completely admit it, but this connection isn't something we will be able to ignore.

When he sinks deep and rolls his hips, I think I am going to pass out. The rings in his dick add to the increasing pleasure, the one hugging my swollen clit sends shocks of pleasure pulsing from my center in waves.

He slows his attack of my mouth and with a few small kisses, pulls back, and looks into my eyes. "Never. Felt. This. Good," he whispers against my lips, his slow thrusting bringing each word home. With one more kiss, he lifts his body from mine and bends his head to look down to where we join. I follow his gaze and watch as he slowly pushes deep, pulls out, and then repeats. There is something so erotic about watching him take me.

When his eyes come back up and meet mine, one side of his mouth lifts and his handsome features relax with pleasure as my body tightens around his. His lets out a strangled moan, closing his eyes slightly. "Love seeing you taking my dick. Soaked, baby." He pulls out, keeping his torturous pace, and pauses briefly before slamming deep. "Goddamn, feels so fucking good."

I vaguely hear the sound again that woke us up in the background, but when his hips rotate, and swirls of ecstasy start to take over my body, my mind no longer cares. My hips rise from the bed to meet his, his hands curl around my shoulders and use his hold to pick up his speed; the pleasure is almost too much to take. I wrap my legs lightly around his back and press my heels into his ass, silently pleading for him to take me even harder.

By the time both climb high and are about to push over, we are both covered in sweat and breathing like we've run a marathon. My fingers claw at his back and his teeth latch to my shoulder. It is raw, hard, and so fucking good that I never want it to end.

"Fuck," he hisses.

"God, YES!" I scream and with a few more rolls of his hips, we both find our release. My vision goes black for a few seconds and those damn angels in heaven are singing again.

He rolls to his back, taking me with him. His breathing is just slowing down when the phone next to his head starts ringing.

"You have got to be fucking kidding me," he rumbles under my ear. Reaching over, he snatches the phone off the cradle and barks a nasty, "What?"

He is silent for a while, offering a few gruff manly grunts and then disconnects. "Gotta take care of this shit real quick, babe," he says softly with only a small bite left to his tone. Apparently, his anger at the caller has diminished slightly. At least he doesn't direct it at me. "Go run a bath and I'll be right back, yeah? Need to go down to the gates and help out a situation."

My body is still enjoying the blissful state he just put me in, so it takes me a second to understand he is leaving. But, he said he would be back, and that is good enough for now.

I roll to my side and watch him hastily pull on some sweats and a faded USMC tee shirt. "Be back, Beauty." With a small smile and a kiss, he takes off out the door. I stretch and look up at the ceiling.

It seems strange that we are this comfortable with each other after only knowing each other for a few days, but there is a connection there that is hard to ignore. Still, a small part of me worries that he might be hiding something. I have spent more years than I can remember during and after Fia's death feeling like all men are evil. But my gut, my gut is telling me to stick this one out… to trust this man. For now, I plan to just enjoy life and live it day to day the best I can.

With a vow to give this guy a chance, I jump out of bed and take off for the promised bath.

CHAPTER 12
Greg

The last thing I want to deal with after what could possibly be the best fucking sex I have ever had in my life is crazy Mandy. It is easy to ignore the phone when I have Melissa's wet, tight heat hugging my dick. There isn't a goddamn thing in the world that could pull me from that. The feel of her body. I have never experienced anything like that, and it is something I'm not willing to give up anytime soon.

I knew when I first saw her that she would be someone worth the trouble, and trouble she is. Fuck. My pants are getting tight just thinking about all that feisty attitude she throws around. The last thing I need when dealing with Mandy and her crazy is a goddamn hard on. She would take that shit as encouragement.

Leaving the house and knowing that Melissa is currently naked and very sated in my bed is hard. I should be worried about the connection being so intense between us but this is what I have been looking for, what I want.

The only problem with that is the potential 'fuck me' she dropped last night. When she told me about her sister, my heart stopped. Right there in my chest, the bastard just skidded to a big fucking halt. Could I be sure? No. Am I pretty fucking positive that her sister was Sofia

Wagner? Yeah. First chance I get I am going to rain a fire storm on Derrick. A son? Not once did he mention she had a kid who survived that shit. Fuck me, he didn't tell me there was a kid at all! Sure, I could blame myself for not checking more into it, but that's what I pay Derrick to do. Simon would know within a second if I were watching him again. Slimy motherfucker.

I have been so consumed with finding some sort of vengeance for Grace that I let it blind me. Axel told me from day one to let one of the other guys take over and be the eyes for me, but it is just too important to me. And in the end, I have nothing to show for it. Grace is gone, Melissa's sister is gone, and that motherfucker got the easy out.

Now, I have to figure out if I can tell Melissa that the man who took her sister, her nephew's mother, is someone I have tried and have been unsuccessful in stopping.

I slam my fist into the steering wheel and start the truck. It doesn't take me long to reach the front gate and see a worried looking Stan.

"Hey man, where is she?"

"Oh hey, Mr. Cage." He is pacing back and forth in his small little house office, clearly shaken by the crazy bitch that has become my shadow. Give a girl some good dick and all of a sudden, they think you have the answers to world peace. "She—she is over there, Mr. Cage. I am so sorry to call so many times, but she wouldn't leave and when she started to try and climb the gate, I didn't know what to do."

"You did the right thing, Stan. Don't worry about her. I'll straighten her out right now, okay?" Poor old guy, thinking he has an easy job to keep him busy between his golf games.

Walking over to the gate entrance, I see her standing by her car with her arms crossed and attitude flying high. What. The. Fuck?

"Amanda." She doesn't even flinch at my biting tone. Not a brow lift, lip curl, nothing. Not a single reaction to the fact I do not want to see her here. "What are you doing here?"

She moves now, pushing herself off her immaculate BMW that I'm sure her daddy bought her, and strutting like the practiced whore she is. "Greg, baby... I knew you would be happy to see me! I wanted to surprise you and bring you breakfast in bed, but that *man* wouldn't let me in. I told him you wouldn't mind, baby."

I look around to see if I can find the hidden cameras that have to be around here somewhere. There is no fucking way this bitch is for real. "What the hell are you talking about, Mandy? Never. I would never give you access to my house like that. You only know where the hell to find me because I was hard up enough for some ass that I brought you here; that was my mistake. You need to go home, Mandy. Go home and forget that you know me." Turning around and walking away from the gate should have been easy, but when I hear a banshee cry, I can't help but turn back around.

To say I was shocked to see her attempting to climb the gate is an understatement. But there she is, all long legs, short skirt, and blonde hair trying to scale the fucking gate. Twilight Zone, that is the only explanation I can even begin to think.

Shaking my head at the absurdity that is Amanda White, I turn and attempt to make my way back to Stan, but before I can even take one step, she is screaming. Not just normal crazy girl screaming, but this shit sounds like it is straight out of the exorcist. I check with Stan before moving back to deal with the nutjob doing her best impression of a monkey on fucking crack. Poor guy looks terrified.

"Mr. Cage? Do-do you need me to call someone?" He steps back into the safety of his little office but holds the phone out the door. "Just let me know, Mr. Cage." And with that, he shuts the door.

Fucking figures. All I want to do is get back to Melissa, but this shit has got to stop.

When she sees me starting back in her direction, she immediately quiets and starts back down. Her shirt is half-unbuttoned, she's missing a shoe, and I'm pretty sure all of her sanity.

"What in the fucking shit do you think you're playing at right now, Mandy?" I growl. My voice sounds about as lethal as I have heard it before, and this is the first time I have ever directed this tone towards a woman. "This isn't what we have and you know it."

"But... baby," she whines, "I saw you last night. During the ceremony, you kept looking right at me. Like you couldn't wait for that to be us. I know you are just playing hard to get right now. It's okay, baby. I know what you really want."

How in the hell is it possible for me to misjudge someone this badly. On a scale of one to ten, this chick is a fifty, and that's being generous, in the off her rocker, needs a white jacket and daily pills fucking crazy.

"Open it up, Stan," I yell over my shoulder. When the gate is open enough for me to slip through, I make my way closer to her. There is no fucking way my face is inviting contact but that doesn't stop her, hell no it doesn't. Apparently, stepping through those gates is my first mistake. Thinking she might have any sanity left is my second. She squeals, like a goddamn seal and launches herself at me.

"Oh, baby! I knew it!" I can feel her ridiculously long nails biting into my neck as she peppers her mouth all over my face. Trying my best to fight the urge to shove her off, and failing rapidly, only fuels my fury.

"Get off me right now." She has her legs wrapped around my hips and doesn't even loosen the grip she has on my head.

"Why, baby? Don't you want to take me back to your place now? We can celebrate!"

"Off. Me. Now."

"Okay, silly! I get it; you don't want anyone to watch. I know how you must want my body for your eyes only."

What the fuck! "Woman, you have lost your fucking mind. Let me clue you in real quick because I have better things to do right now. Going to be clear as I can fucking be so there is no goddamn room for your head to twist this shit into something it isn't. Something it sure as shit will never be. First, I damn sure wasn't looking at you yesterday. Who I was looking at isn't your fucking business, but I can assure you *she* knows that it was *her* my eyes couldn't leave. Second, this is not hard to get. This right here, this is me trying to get the hell away. And last, I do not want you anywhere near my bed. What I want is back at my house keeping the sheets warm until I get back. What I want is so far from what this bullshit is. Hear this, Mandy; you were convenient. I needed something that you offered and never made promises to you for anything else. Don't. Fuck. With. Me."

A wise man would anticipate the claws to the face, but I am too busy thinking about getting her gone and getting back to my house that her slap is the last thing I see coming. Her fake as fuck act slips, and I swear the devil is looking back at me. I bring my hand up and wipe off the blood I can feel trailing down my cheek. This will be fun to explain to Melissa.

"What we had was real, and you felt it! I won't let anyone stand in the way of what I want. How about you hear that, Greg!"

"Are we even on the same fucking planet right now? I don't fucking want you, Mandy! Never made the promise of more, and you fucking know it." She doesn't even flinch when I get in her space. She has no fear, or maybe she has a death wish. "If you even think about going near my girl I will make your life a nightmare." And with that, I turn and walk back through the gate. Should have been watching my back though because taking a stiletto in the shoulder blade is no a fucking picnic.

"You'll regret this, Greg!"

I wait for the gate to close up before walking over to Stan. "Sorry about that. You call me if you see her again, yeah?"

"Yes, oh… yes, Mr. Cage." He nods his old weathered head so quickly I am slightly worried he might hurt himself.

"Enjoy the day, Stan. Sorry about that little interruption."

I take the long way back, taking a few extra roads to try and calm down. I had really hoped to enjoy the day with Melissa, get to know her better, without the real word fucking with us. Unfortunately, I get to go back and explain why I have claw marks on my face, and I smell like a two-cent whore.

Fucking lovely.

Melissa

I hear the door chime but don't move a muscle from the warm bath. It's been years since I have enjoyed this luxury. I am so used to my rusty, water stained one stall shower that I might never leave this room.

"Beauty?"

"In here!" I answer with a small smile curving my lips. Who would have thought that nickname would be growing on me.

"Goddamn…" He rumbles behind my shoulder. I plaster on the most seductive smile I have in my bag of tricks and turn my head. The smile and invitation to join dies on my lips.

"What the fuck happened to you?" He not only looks like he just fought a bear and lost, but you can tell the lighthearted mood we both woke up with is long gone. "Are you okay?"

"I am now," he replies softly. I watch in stunned silence as he begins pulling off his clothes. When he walks over and stands next to the tub, I lick my lips.

"I can see that. Why don't we talk about why your face looks like that and you have red lipstick all over your face?" I should be pissed but curiosity seems to be winning this emotional round.

"Son of a bitch!" he hisses. "Babe, let me in so I can feel you against me."

Okay, I can't argue with that, but I want answers first. "I don't think so, stud. Talk."

"Fucking hell, you can bust my balls any day, but let me feel you against me, babe. I need that to help calm me the hell down." He climbs over the edge and settles himself before pulling my back to his front, and rubbing his hands across every inch of my skin he can reach.

"I hate to point out the obvious, big boy, but it doesn't seem to be working," I tell him when I feel his hard length against my back.

"Mmm, no it doesn't." He agrees with a few kisses to my neck. "I would rather not have this conversation, but since it literally knocked on the gate this morning, we have no choice. Understand I won't keep shit from you and this is no different, but I didn't want to start this with something nasty."

"And what exactly are we starting?" I ask.

"Don't play games right now, Melissa. Babe, you know just as good as I do that me and you are happening. This isn't some cheap thrill. You feel it, but if you need me to remind you, just let me know."

"Yeah, maybe when you finish telling me about the trip out this morning."

"Right. Blondie from the club and church yesterday? Apparently, when I told her that the only thing she ever was to me was a number in my phone, I wasn't clear enough. She showed up this morning, about gave the morning gatekeeper a heart attack with her shit. I reminded her, again, that her and I were never anything and wouldn't ever be something."

"I'm guessing the claws weren't part of your end game?" I turn and kneel in front of him. With one hand to his chin, I move his head to give me a better look at the angry red welts on his skin. "Do you need a rabies shot?"

I am so busy looking at the marks, and trying to decide if he needs antibiotics or something stronger, that the rough, deep laugh that bursts from his lips catches me off guard.   I jump slightly, correcting myself before my knees can do some serious damage to his manhood.

"No, babe. No shots. Although, if you want to play nurse, I won't argue."

"Shut up," I laugh. "Seriously, do you need me to rough her up?"

"Jesus, you're serious right now, aren't you?" He quickly sobers when he sees that I will, in fact, go offer up a good twat punch or two. "Babe, I got this. If you see her, do not even go near her. If I'm not there, call me. I would say I don't think she will be an issue, but after her little stunt this morning, I'm not really sure what she will do next. I can promise you, there is no fucking way she misunderstood me this time."

"Let's hope so. I don't share. Never learned."

"Never shared? Jesus, you kill me. Now, come here and kiss me and make it better."

He wraps his arms around my waist and pulls me closer. Our lips seal together, and I immediately respond to this man. By the time I finish 'making it better', there's more water on the floor than is left in the tub. But, I climb out of that tub with some serious satisfaction that some psycho ex hasn't ruined the morning.

CHAPTER 13
Melissa

True to his word, we spend the whole day Sunday wrapped up in each other. The times we manage to come up for air to refuel only end up with even more incredible sex in random spots around his house. I don't want the day to end, but with Monday morning coming quicker than I wish, I know I have to get home.

"Stay," he mumbles into my neck when I try to leave the bed. I am sore in places I have never been sore before. It is the best feeling.

"Can't. I have to be in at 7:00." I am trying, unsuccessfully, to leave his warm cocoon of sex.

"Leave in the morning," he replies, while snaking his hand down my body and over my wet lips. "Stay."

"Greg, really. I can't stay, I have to be up, and I actually have to get some sleep to get up."

His fingers stop their movement, and within seconds, I'm on my back with his hard body over mine. "Come back tomorrow?" His blue eyes are searching mine, and there isn't anything but unspoken promise reflecting in them. "Come on, Beauty." His hips start rubbing against mine. With each thrust forward, the metal through his dick hits my clit, and send shocks through my body, electrifying my skin and burning my blood. "If you won't stay, at least say goodbye right."

This man… it is glorious to knock him down a few notches on the ego scale. Watching his eyes spark when I give him a hard push off of me, then and jump on top is priceless.

"What did you have in mind?" I ask, rubbing my swollen sex against his hard body. "Did you want a goodnight kiss?"

"Yeah, Beauty, give me a goodnight kiss, and I might let you leave."

With a laugh that is too loud even to my ears, I slide my hands up his corded arms and pull his arms above his head. "Don't move."

Leaning up, I run my hands down his hard chest, leaving red lines where my nails pass over his heated skin. Not hard enough to hurt, but it's enough to make him feel the bite. "Ready for your kiss?" He's close to snapping, and I fucking love it. Without giving him any warning to my intentions, I crawl off his body. He raises one dark brow as I kneel close to his shoulder. "Pucker up, *babe*," I say, and with a little twisting and maneuvering, bring my *lips* to his, and my mouth wraps tight around his throbbing dick.

I lean up slightly when I feel his large hands grab my hips and pull me closer to his mouth, his fingers digging into my skin to make sure he doesn't lose his hold.

"You aren't following the rules." I joke.

He gives me a sharp bite against my pussy, lifts his mouth off just enough to speak, and grunts, "Fuck the rules. Goddamn you taste so fucking good."

When he brings his lips back and clamps down, I moan like a whore and bring my lips back down to his cock. The rings throw me for a second until I learn how to work them, and more importantly, how he likes me to work them. When I flick the ring through the tip, he moans. When I put my lips around both piercings and swirl my tongue, his whole body jerks and he growls against my clit. He almost flies off the bed when I take him deep in my throat and swallow around the tip.

"Fuck!" he roars against my skin, turning his head and biting down against my thigh. The only thing he does is fuel my desire. I take him as deep as I can before slowly dragging my mouth back up. "Meliiii…," he trails off and after a few seconds of feeling his abs clench against my tits, he brings his mouth to my wet center again and digs in.

We continue to duel against each other for a good ten minutes, silently daring the other to come first, but when he takes one of the hands tightly gripping me, and runs a finger lightly across my ass, I know I won't last long. He trails his finger from each end until he sinks it deep. With just a few deep stabs, I'm coming against his tongue. I pull my mouth free and scream loudly.

"You… God… shit." He laughs lightly against my pulsing core, and before I can bring my mouth back down to his swollen length, he has me flying through the air and on my back in seconds.

"Can't go slow, babe; you have me strung too tight."

"Condom, Greg."

"Fuck, I want to feel you." I know what he means; I would love to feel him bare.

"You go make sure bitch-face Barbie hasn't passed some nasty crotch rot off on you, and you're more than welcome to it, but not until you get checked. Firm on that, Greg."

He grumbles his way to the drawer that has fallen to the floor at some point during the day, scattering condoms across the room, pick one up, and in no time is pushing hard back into me.

Frantic would be a good word to describe how we come together. Our skin slick with sweat, slapping together. Nails biting into skin, and fingers digging deep. Lips colliding and moans dancing together.

It is magical.

"You sure you have to go?" He asks me from his position sprawled naked on the bed. My eyes zone in on his naked skin, wishing I didn't have to leave but knowing I need to. I feel the connection, but I know we are moving way too fast. A little distance will be a good thing. Who knows, we might wake up in the morning and wonder what the hell has gotten into us. Doubtful, but it might happen.

"Yeah. I've got some things to take care of tonight, and then I have to go see Cohen tomorrow."

"Nephew, right."

"Oh my God! You're jealous of a kid? That's a good one." I burst out laughing when he looks away, clearly embarrassed by his jealousy.

"Come over Tuesday. We can do dinner or something," he throws back at me after a few moments of silence.

"Maybe," I smile over at him and zip the back of my dress. Nothing like stepping into the previous days clothing. "I'll call you."

"Melissa, babe... that sounds like one hell of a brush off." He runs his hand through his hair and looks me in the eye. "Don't play that hard ass shit; you feel it, this connection we have isn't going anywhere."

"Fuck that." He pushes off the bed and stalks over to me. It's hard to remember my reasons for wanting to keep this just sex. Just amazing, mind-blowing sex, when he is standing in front of me completely naked. "I won't let you keep running when this feels so right." His voice rings out strong and firm.

"It's impossible to have a serious conversation with you when your dick is bobbing all over the place. Want to put some pants on?" He just continues to burn his gaze all over my face, refusing to let my sorry attempt at changing the subject work. "You scare me," I whisper.

His eyes lose their hard, demanding look, and he immediately softens. "Beauty," he murmurs back, "just give it a try. You don't get a connection like ours and just throw it away. Just try."

It's moments like this, moments when all I want to do is be anyone other than the strong one, when I swear I can hear my sister speaking to me. Yelling at me to *live*. Yelling at me to stop letting *her* life and *her* mistakes pave the way for my happiness. The way to own my life and not let it be owned.

"Yeah... I can try."

"Tuesday?" He asks again.

"Tuesday." I echo.

I pull up at my apartment complex and sit in my car just taking in the lush 'ghetto-ness' of my life. I hate living here. Having spent the last day in Greg's world, this is the last place that I want to be. I'm pretty sure there is a homeless man sleeping on the corner of my building and I'm fairly positive that the apartment across from mine is running some massive drug warehouse.

With a deep sigh, I drag myself out of the car and make my way up to my apartment. Passing the drunk unconscious man in the bushes and the neighbor's door that smells like a pot factory, I curse my financial status while throwing the door closed and locking all seven locks. I'm not paranoid, just smart.

Not surprising, the message light is blinking; I'm shocked that my house phone wasn't ringing constantly all weekend. I realized too late Saturday that I had left my cell at home. With a mother like mine, that isn't something you want to do. Having already lost Fia, she tends to go into crazy mode when she can't get ahold of me after too long.

I toss my keys and purse down on the counter, before pressing play and settling in for a good time.

"Meli-Kate, where are you, baby? Cohen misses you. Call me baby." My mother's voice echoes through the room, making me feel slightly guilty for not being home when she called.

"Meli-Kate, where are you? Call me." Not even an hour later.

"Meli, baby? Please call me... you know I will worry." At least she waited until Saturday night for that one.

Five more messages and the increasing unease that laces her tone has me reaching for the phone until the last one begins playing. Her words immediately stop me.

"Melissa. Baby, they're at it again. I don't know where you are, but they sent another letter." Click. She doesn't need to say more because I know exactly *who* she is talking about and I know exactly *who* they want.

"Fuck," I hiss, quickly picking up the phone and calling my mother.

"Baby, where have you been?" she rushes out. Not even a full ring and she has the phone in her hands.

"Jesus, Mom, I told you I had the wedding for my friend and wouldn't be around this weekend."

"I know, I know. I'm sorry but you should keep your cell phone on you." She takes a deep breath and seems to hold it for hours before letting it out in a rush. "They're at it again, Meli."

"What did the letter say this time?" I question.

"Susan claims that with my old age, and with you working too many hours to care for Cohen, that she should have sole custody. She claims that Sofia's will was incorrect and that Simon wouldn't have ever agreed to that, regardless of the fact that his signature is on the contract."

"How can she argue that son of a bitch didn't agree with it when Fia had all the proper paperwork drawn up? She wasn't stupid, mom. She knew what would happen if Susan got her hands on him."

"I know. She isn't going to stop easily, Melissa. She wants him. I don't know why she is so determined, when best I can tell she didn't give two shakes about her own son. Probably why he ended up crazy and possessed." I can hear her starting to lose her patience.

"She won't get him." I promise. No way in hell, I would snatch him up, and run off to Mexico quicker than she can blink.

"Come over tomorrow? I need to see you; he needs to see you. I would feel better with my baby home with me."

I laugh but it holds no humor.

"Alright. I'll tell Dr. Shannon that I can't stay late and come over for dinner."

"Love you to pieces, Meli-Kate."

"Love you too, Mom."

That night, nightmares of Fia's life, her insane mother-in-law, and shadows stealing my nephew haunt me until the light of dawn filters through my shades. My blissful weekend and the man that has wedged himself in my heart after such a short time are long forgotten.

CHAPTER 14
Greg

For the last two years, I have watched one of the most important people in my life find herself, and then find love. After that, I started second-guessing everything that I thought I was okay with in life. A relationship was never something I wanted; I was happy to spend my time with bitches like Mandy.

Well, that might be a stretch. I have definitely misjudged her, big fucking time. Watching Izzy and Axel find each other again and overcome so much shit to be together, makes me crave what they have. I want someone to lift me up, someone to go home to, and someone to have children with. I am ready, and for the first time in my life, I have a woman I feel might be worth making those changes for.

I won't go so far as saying it was love at first sight, but it damn sure was hard on at first sight. That motherfucker doesn't have selective taste though, so I can't rely on that alone.

The first time she opened her mouth and started throwing her attitude, is when I knew that she is worth it. She won't be easy. I know that she's hesitant to start something and I am willing to bet it isn't because of someone burning her. When she told me about her sister, and I realized just whom she is connected to, I knew... I knew whatever issues she has are because of that motherfucker.

Simon-fucking-Wagner.

The reason I don't have Grace by my side anymore is the same fucking reason she doesn't have her sister. I am man enough to admit that it worries me about what will happen when she finds out about that connection.

Monday morning comes way too fucking soon. I have spent the night hugging the pillow that still smells of my Beauty like a little bitch. Every time the scent of vanilla hits my system, it is like a signal straight to my dick to salute the heavens. Every dream is about her. How her blue eyes spark with fire and lust. How they go wide and lost there when she comes. And how when she forgets to be scared, she gazes at me like she knows I hold all the answers.

Yeah, I am officially hooked.

A clear sign of my distraction is my missing Sway's presence when I pull up at Corps Security. I am busy picturing Melissa bent over my kitchen counter, but when I look up and see Swag waving like an idiot, the hard on I have been sporting all morning dies a quick death.

What the fuck?

Over the last few years that I have known this man, I have learned he is as unpredictable as they come. But the sight that meets me this morning is like nothing he has ever done before. There he is, standing on the sidewalk wearing those camouflage skintight pants things that chicks wear. The ones that make a man fall all over himself to follow her ass around the world, but on this man, they might scar me for life. If that isn't enough, the sparkling burgundy shirt hugging his round stomach might get a good laugh. Then, I notice what he is doing.

"Sway? Why are you painting the sidewalk?" I question, looking down into the bucket of golden *shining* paint, "Is that fucking glitter?"

"Don't you start with all your alpha hotness, Gregory. Of course, this is glitter! You can't paint the sidewalk gold without glitter!" He's serious, bobbing his head left and right, and waving his hands all over the place.

"This is for real? You're painting the sidewalk fucking gold? Does Axel know about this shit?"

"Of course he does, my king of hotness. Don't be such a tight ass. Actually, never mind that darlin', be a tight ass... just let me see it." He starts laughing like a loon and all I can do is look around and notice the explosion of fucking *glitter*.

"Sway, my man, you wouldn't know what to do with me." He sobers instantly and I kick myself for encouraging him. "Forget I said that. Tell me *why* you feel the need to throw glitter all over the damn place?"

"Because my hunk of fine, glitter makes everyone happy!" When he starts dancing around his paint bucket, I have to leave. There is only so much Sway that I can handle when he is acting like this. I might joke, but that man is the funniest little shit I have ever met.

"Right. You know who loves glitter?" I question, noticing Coop's jeep pulling in. "Coop loves glitter. Why don't you go give him a good morning that will make his day, Sway? I'll even hold your brush."

"Ohhh! Yes, right away, Sir Sex-o-lot!" He bends over, grabs a handful of glitter, and runs across the lot as fast as his heels will take him. I can see Coop's eyes widen when he takes in the man running full speed at him.

At this point, I couldn't stop laughing if I try. The second Coop steps out of the out of the jeep, Sway attacks, throwing glitter in the air and screaming 'good morning'. When he leaps into Coop's arms, I fear I might hurt something, laughing as hard as I am.

"Good morning, asshole!" I yell over at Coop and make my way inside.

"What the hell is going on out there?" Beck asks, stepping up to the front window. When he sees Coop trying to untangle himself from Sway, he throws his head back and his laughter booms through the room, causing Emmy to jump in her seat behind the front desk.

"You are all so immature." I hear her mumble under her breath.

"Cheer up, Em. It's only Monday... way too soon for that."

When I see the look in her eye that clearly screams 'don't mess with me', I make quick work at heading to my office and a mental note to find out what is weighing on her mind.

First thing I need to handle is calling that bastard Derrick. Rounding my desk, I slam my body down and listen to the legs of my chair protest before picking up the phone and dialing a number that I won't forget. After all, when you call it daily for almost two years, you don't forget that shit easily.

"Johnson," he says in an impatient tone.

"Derrick." My tone is lethal. This jerkoff knows I am not a man to cross.

"C-Cage," he sputters, clears his throat and tries again, "Cage, how can I help you?"

"First thing you can do is tell me if you just conveniently forgot to mention that Simon and Sofia Wagner have a son, a son that is very much alive?"

"*Shit,*" he hisses, panic taking over his carefree fake bullshit.

"And by shit, I hope to fuck that means you must have misplaced your fucking brain and common sense? Do you not think that would be something, I don't know, the person signing your goddamn checks to investigate that bastard should know?" My raised voice must have alerted Axel that shit is going down. Before I can even finish speaking, he is walking in, shutting the door, and taking a seat across from me.

"Look, Cage. Man, I didn't think it was a big deal. The kid was fine. It sucks about his parents, but he went to the chick's mom. It was all good."

The growl that erupts from my throat is feral enough to scare any motherfucker. "That kid has a name, asshole. You better fucking send me full case files. Today. I don't give a fucking shit if you have to rent a goddamn bike and pedal you ass over here. One hour. I want everything you didn't fucking share with me a year ago!" Slamming the phone down should give me some satisfaction, but the rage boiling inside me just keeps heating up.

"You want to talk about it?" Axel questions.

"You want to tell me why the hell you're here when you should be at home with your bride?" Changing the subject seems wise with the amount of anger I'm dealing with.

"You try staying at home when you are attacked every two seconds! That woman is insatiable. Never thought I would need a break, but my dick is tired man."

"Jesus Christ, jackass. Can you not talk about that shit with me?"

"You asked." He laughed.

"The fuck I did. I asked why you're here, not why your dick isn't working."

"Right, enough about my wife. Want to tell me now what that was all about?" All the humor leaves his face. I can tell he is worried.

"You know Izzy's friend, the nurse at Nate's doctor's place?"

"Yeah, what about her?" He questions, looking at me as if I did something wrong. "Jesus, tell me you haven't made her your new plaything."

"Do *not* fucking call her a plaything," I growl at him. His eyes narrow at my tone and I would laugh if I weren't still heated over the plaything comment.

"Okay. You want to explain that shit? I've never seen you two seconds from pissing all over the place to mark your territory." He lets out a laugh and holds his hands up.

Do I really want to get into this with Axel? Sure, out of the five of us, he would be the one with the experience to tell me what I need to do, but having him know what a whipped bitch I am over one chick I just met is something different.

"Nothing to tell, yet."

"And 'yet' means you took her home with you after the wedding. Let me guess. Spent the weekend together. Decided you want to run off into the fucking sunset and have little dogs that yap at the mailman. Maybe if you're lucky, find a bowling league that meets every Friday. What the fuck man, this timid shit isn't like you."

"Fuck you, asshole!" I chunk an unopened pack of computer paper and laugh when it knocks him in the head. "You deserved that."

"What the fuck ever. Izzy is going to have your ass for messing with my perfection." He throws the package back on the desk and gives me one of his silent 'you better start talking' looks. Jesus Christ. He's about to go all Dr. Phil. "What's going on, G? You've been around but silent ever since Nate was born. I know something happened with that motherfucker your sister was married to, but you never wanted to talk. So... now you're going to."

"Would you like me to go put my fucking vagina on for this talk?" Sarcasm is dripping from my words. I need to hash this out, but fuck, this is awkward. Not many people know the details on Grace. Well, I should say the 'after' Grace. Axel told me over and over to let it go, to live the life Grace would want for me... but I can't. I need to see Simon brought to justice. He didn't get the justice I would have chosen, but I'm crying into my milk and cookies that he is rotting in hell either.

"No need to be an asshole, Greg. Just want to know how I can help." He leans back in the chair, and I can tell he means it. Axel would catch hell from Izzy for not helping me, but more importantly, he is family. And family helps family.

With a deep breath, I let the story out. "Her sister was married to Simon. Didn't know for sure until this morning, but after that call to Derrick, I sure do. The worst part, I don't know how she'll handle it when I tell her I could have stopped him, but I didn't." I rest my head forward on my hands and let out a heavy sigh, "I could have stopped him, and she wouldn't have lost her sister. Holding that shit heavy, Ax."

After a long period of silence, he speaks and I can tell by his tone that what I just put out there shocks him. "I don't even know what is the most fucked up part of all that. The fact that there is this messed up connection between the two of you or that you actually blame yourself for that shit that happened. You know just as well as I do that there wasn't anything you could have done to that bastard. You didn't have any proof, Greg. Nothing. You can't keep blaming yourself for something that you couldn't control."

"The hell I couldn't! I could have taken his ass out a long time ago, and you know it."

"And what? Spent the next lifetime locked up? You know Grace wouldn't have wanted that life for you, Greg. You know she would want you to be happy." His eyes have that look that he used to give Izzy when she would go back into herself. The look she got when she remembered that I almost died to save her. The same thing I should have been able to do for Grace and Sofia. I hate being on the receiving end of that look.

"How am I supposed to tell her that I not only know who her nephew's father is, but that I tried and failed to find something to put him away before he fucked up another woman?" Frustration doesn't even come close to how I feel right now. I know that what I've found with Melissa is worth exploring, and I will be damned if I let Simon fuck with that from the grave.

"Don't tell her right away, man. You just met, and if you are serious about her and this relationship, you need to find out if it's worth it. Because you know that no matter how you lay that out there, she isn't going to take it well. She needs to know you first. But, don't let this sit too long, Greg; it'll be worse and it might not be fixable."

"I hear you, but I don't like the idea of starting something new on a foundation that isn't solid." I lean back in my chair and look him in the eye. "I feel it Ax, that connection that you can't ignore. And I want it."

His eyes widen slightly, but before he can speak, we hear a commotion coming from the front.

"What the hell happened to you?" We hear a bellow from the front of the office, followed by Coop's cackles down the hall.

"Shut up!" Maddox's lethal tone cuts him silent.

The sight that greets Axel and me when we reach the lobby is one that has me struggling with my own laughter.

There stands Maddox Locke, all six-foot-four inches of pissed off and rumpled man. The best part is the gold paint and glitter covers every inch of his body from his hair to his boots.

"You look ridiculous," I laugh, unable to control it.

"Did you tell Mr. Happiness next door to make a golden brick road out there?" He starts walking over to me and I notice his slight limp, which sobers my humor instantly.

"You okay?" He doesn't miss my question but ignores me and stalks off to the back of the office.

Looking over at Axel, he catches my concern and takes off to make sure everything is okay with Maddox. It might be funny, but in all seriousness, we all worry about him. Looking over at Coop to make sure he is keeping his shit in check, I find him following Axel into the back.

"Em babe, where is Beck?" She looks up and I can't help but notice the pain in her eyes. "Em? What's going on?"

"Nothing, Greg. I'm fine. Beck left about five minutes before Maddox got here. He was going to check on some cases," she says. She clears her throat and her eyes are begging me to stop, pleading with me to not ask any more questions.

"Emmy. You know my history and you know I am here for you, so please tell me what has taken your smile." The guys take great pleasure in making fun of how much I father these girls, but when it comes down to it, I can't stomach the thought that someone is hurting them. I made a vow to myself a few years after I lost Grace, after too many years of careless and reckless abandon, that I would never let anything happen to another woman in my life.

"It really is nothing. Okay?" She sighs, "Let's just say it was made painfully clear that I will never be what *he* wants." She doesn't need to say more for me to know that the *he* is the one and only Maddox Locke. Poor girl has had it bad for him for too long.

"Emmy, you do know it isn't anything about you, right?" I round the desk and kneel in front of her, spinning the chair so that I can look her in the eye. "Sometimes there is nothing you can do, no matter how pure your heart is, to clear the darkness from someone's past. He's got some shit that would even dim your light, babe. Leave it and just be there for him if he asks, yeah?" It doesn't sit well with me that this sweet and innocent woman has her sights set on Maddox, the one we have dubbed 'the dark one' for years.

"I understand, Greg. It's just not easy." Watching the single tear fall from her golden eye is a killer. Slowly over the months, she has gone from smiling freely and shyly to being as stoic as Maddox.

"Nothing worth having ever is, babe." When my own words smack me in the face I realize that to make things happen with Melissa, I'm going to need to eat those words.

CHAPTER 15
greg

Once things settle at the office, it is a lot easier to go about my business. My fire at Derrick hasn't dimmed one bit, but I know I need to keep my head straight here. Not even thirty minutes after my call, Derrick comes running into the building with a box full of case files. I'm pretty sure the idiot pissed his pants when he walked in my office and found not only one pissed off person but two more. Coop and Axel have no issues with sitting in here and throwing their vibes at the idiot.

It takes me a good hour to look over the case files and realize that I have messed up and messed up big in trusting him. Not only is he lacking on the information he has relayed to me but he has also failed to mention just how bad things had been in the Wagner house. I find five trips to the hospital, not including the birth of the son I never knew about, fourteen visits from the local police from calls the neighbors had placed that only ended with Sofia Wagner telling them everything was a-fuckin-okay. And the cherry on the top is the final call from Derrick that fails to mention the sleeping son found just upstairs from his dead parents.

"Fuck," I grind out, slamming the latest file of fucked up bullshit down on my desk. "Do you believe this shit?" I ask Maddox. Since I started to pore over the files, he is the only one left in the building stupid enough to put up with my shit. "How could I have been so fucking blind to this shit? I am the one who asked this idiot to investigate, to let me know *everything* and I get half-truths and watered down bullshit."

"Got played. Can't blame yourself for the move he made. You had enough shit on your hands with Izzy, Axel and that motherfucking Brandon." He finishes up looking at the last file I threw at him and leans back in the chair, absentmindedly rubbing his left knee.

"You alright?" I ask, nodding my head towards his knee.

"Fine, shut up about it. I'll be picking glitter out of my brain for years." I can tell there is more there but I know better than to push him on it.

"I'm here if you want to talk. And stop being a son of a bitch, yeah? I'll stay out of your shit, but stop, and you know damn well who I'm talking about here. Now, back to this mess. What do I do with all of this?"

"Keep it close until you know more about this chick. No need to open old wounds unless you know it's worth being the rock she's going to need." He stands up and makes his way over to the door. When he turns around and I meet his black eyes, for the first time in years, I see some compassion in them. "For what it's worth, you deserve some peace, brother. She could be the rock you need too." And with that, he's gone.

I stay in the office for a few more hours catching up on some cases that need some work done, checking in with the ones that need my attention, and just avoiding thinking about Melissa for a few seconds. Not easy, when all I can remember is the weekend I spent with her. All it takes is one second of her face filtering through my mind for my pants to tighten up. To say I've got it bad would be like saying the sun is a small star.

Deciding that I could care less what it says about me to be calling this soon, I pick up my phone and hit her name.

After a few rings, I hear her breathless voice and my heart picks up speed instantly.

"Hello?"

"Melissa." God, just her voice is enough to wipe all the shit from the day away.

"Greg," I might be imagining things, but I'm pretty sure she just sighed my name, and that's enough for my ego to blow up. Yeah, she might play a mean game of keep away, but she isn't as unaffected as she initially wanted me to believe.

"Been a long day, babe, and it's only lunch. Run away with me and let's go grab some."

"That would be nicer than my current plans. I can't get away today, Greg. And I'm not sure about tomorrow."

If it wasn't for the regret in her voice, I might feel like she was giving me the brush off.

"What's going on, Melissa?"

"Nothing you need to worry about, just some family issues." I know it's early and my trust hasn't been earned yet, but that shit still stings a little. I can't help it. It's who I am, and I want to fix things for her.

"You do know you can talk to me. I get you don't want me in your business until you know me better, but if you need to talk, don't shut me out."

There's a long silence, and I can almost hear the wheels turning over the line, "I know. I just need to deal with this, okay?"

I might not like it, but for now, I can give her that. "Yeah, Beauty... for now."

"You're so frustrating, Greg Cage." At least the laughter and lightness I left her with has returned.

"I want to see you soon, and I won't take no for an answer. Finish your family business but call me tomorrow. I don't hear from you tomorrow then I will come to you. Lunch, dinner, or fucking brunch."

"Okay, okay. I'll call you tomorrow and let you know what's going on. Does that work for you?" Smartass temptress.

The next day isn't much better on my sanity. Walking into work on a golden sidewalk is almost comical enough that I might have started the day positively. But entering the office to find Emmy in tears, Coop frustrated with his not knowing shit about women or how to fix them, Beck worrying and consoling Emmy, and Maddox punching holes in his office, doesn't bode for a good beginning.

I feel torn between my need to protect Emmy and her innocent, pure love for a man who can't accept it, and a man who has been a brother to me for many years. I know the background and I know that it isn't going to get better anytime soon.

With Axel finally gone for the week, all the heavy shit falls straight on my shoulders. The best anyone can get out of Emmy is that she is okay. She calms down when I pull her aside and remind her of our previous conversation. I get her, I really do. Some of us are put on this earth to heal, to make others' lives brighter, and when those people don't want our help, our love? We feel it deep. No matter what I say, that isn't going to change with her but this discord in the office needs to fucking stop.

After that, it seems like fire after fire. We have cases with issues, computers crashing, and Maddox still banging shit around in his office. If I know I am going to see Melissa today, I can almost take this shit, but already knowing that isn't going to be happening is just increasing my foul mood.

By mid-afternoon, I can't take it anymore and finally call her. I get her voicemail and leave a quick message to call. Her return text is short and to the point, **'Can't do today, too much family stuff.'**, and has my gut rolling. No reason, but my gut never lets me down. Something is going on and I can't help her without knowing *what* is happening.

This feeling of not helping is new to me. For the last almost five years, I have been the rock, the go to, the strength to help, and it almost makes me feel like I am doing something that would make Grace proud of me. Something better than all those years that I spent wasting away, living off booze, and whores on the road.

I want to be that person for Melissa, and it is killing me that she won't let me in. My mind keeps telling me to be patient, it's new, and who trusts someone that much after a week? But my heart, fuck me, my heart is telling me to drive over to her now and demand she let me in.

Crazy, I know this… but when you know, you know. She is a woman worth the trouble and if my gut is right, she could be the one to heal the wounds I have been carrying around for far too long.

When my phone rings right before closing time and I see Melissa's name across the screen, my heart leaps. Like a little bitch, it leaps right into my throat. One week and I am already this deep, shit.

"Miss me?" Expecting to get some kind of sass back or at the very least a hello, the soft sob that catches over the line has my heart dropping right back down. "Melissa? What is it?" Grabbing my keys without even knowing where I am needed is a knee-jerk reaction. I am out the door with a few jerks of my chin to the others, and leaving the lot. "Baby, where are you?"

She takes a few minutes to control herself and when she speaks, the tone isn't sadness. It's pure fury. "I will kill that little tramp, Greg. My car might be shit to someone but it is *mine* and it is important to *me*. Sure it's a piece of shit but it is MY piece of shit!"

At this point, I have to pull over. Despite the driving need to reach her and fix whatever the hell just went down, I can't for the life of me figure out what the hell she is talking about.

'Babe, I'm trying to figure out what exactly you're talking about here, so can you give me some more details?" I lean forward and try to rub some of the stress out of my neck.

"Okay. Let me spell this out in a way you might get. Your little stalker? I'm thinking maybe you weren't clear enough with her when you ended things. I would like to think I know you well enough that you wouldn't be messing with me and trying this hard to get me to open up. So imagine my shock when she shows up at my job throwing her shit!"

Jesus Christ. "Tell me you're kidding right now, Melissa."

"Do you think I would be calling you right now to come get this trash if I wasn't serious?!" Her screams through the line almost cause me to drop the phone.

"Where are you?"

"At the office, you know, my job where there are children and families and all these happy family vibes? Yeah, those vibes just blew the fuck up when 'Stalker Sue' came into my work screaming about how much of a whore I am for breaking up her relationship! THEN when we finally get her out of the office and I have some time to calm down, I walk outside and find her SLICING MY TIRES with a goddamn knife! So, being that I can't drive with FOUR flat tires, I am still at work."

How did I not see *this* coming? Well, maybe not this, but damn Mandy and her fucked up shit.

"Call the police baby; I'll be there in fifteen. And, Melissa?"

"What?" she spits out.

"Might not be the best time to mention this, but all this fire and attitude you're throwing at me? Baby, you got me so worked up that it will be a miracle not to take you the second I lock eyes with yours."

"You're a beast, Greg Cage."

Might have been inappropriate, but when I hear her laughter before disconnecting, I know I did something right today.

CHAPTER 16
Melissa

No need in denying it. Since leaving Greg's house Sunday night, I have been on cloud nine. Not even the crap Cohen's paternal grandmother is throwing our way is messing with my high. I am stressed but only because my mother is making me that way.

Susan has started with her letters again, and has followed those quickly with her calls. And then we get to experience the pleasure of her knocking my mother's door down around three this morning.

A little history of Susan Wagner is helpful. Susan Wagner is a pill poppin', body using, drunk, white trash bitch. She has enough DUIs that she is no longer 'allowed' to drive, but that doesn't stop her. I'm sure at this point that even she has a few venereal diseases. And when she throws her creepy-as-hell wicked witch grin out, all that you see is gums. The only thing Simon Wagner did right in his life was to make sure that Cohen would go to my mother if anything ever happened to them. As fucked up as he was, she is a million times worse.

So, not only is my much needed sleep interrupted by a frantic phone call, AND having to drag myself over to my mother's house to deal with Susan in her drunken rage, but now I have to deal with another crayon not bright enough for the box.

When I find myself pulled, literally pulled, out of the exam room by a furious Dr. Shannon, the last thing I expect to find is the chick that has become my shadow ever since Greg has started showing interest in me. Except this time, she has lost all of her carefully crafted 'perfection'. She looks unkempt. That perfectly put together look I have seen every other time is gone. Poof, and in its place is a complete stranger. She reminds me of one of those stray dogs you see in city alleyways. The ones that have fought over the last scrap of meat for so long that they don't even know a crumb from a pebble. Apparently, Greg is the piece of meat in this equation.

"You fucking bitch!" She screams at the top of her lungs in a waiting room full of patients. Not just patients, but also parents and children of all ages. With her burst of crazy, the small children start getting scared, the older ones get curious, and the parents get pissed. I can already tell that this isn't going to end well.

I lose track of the things she spews across the waiting room. I catch 'bitch' a few more times, 'home wrecker' (which throws me for a loop) but 'whore' is the one that made me snap. I do what I have to do, and that is round the desk, grab her by her bony arm, and lead her to the door. Not a single word passes from my lips, but at this point, I am boiling with anger, and I know the second my lips part, I will enter Crazytown with her.

I open the lobby door and push her out as hard as I can, taking great pleasure in watching her wobble on her heels before falling flat on her ass. She opens her mouth to start another attack of her verbal vomit, but with deadly calm, I force out a firm 'don't', and close the door.

I make the walk of shame past the patients and apologize profusely for the incident. The kids seem to have already forgotten the mad woman and quickly turn their attention back to the Disney movie playing, but the parents look at me with an expression that can't be described as anything other than hate.

When I enter the back office, Dr. Shannon is waiting. I get a box thrust into my arms, and a 'get out, you're fired' before he turns on his old as dirt legs and walks away.

"You can't fire me for someone else's actions! This is ridiculous!" I call after him.

"That's where you are wrong, Melissa. You brought that disturbance into my office and caused a nice big scene that I now have to clean up. Pack your locker up. We will mail your last check."

It takes me a few minutes to really understand that I just lost not only my job, but also the only source of income keeping my mother, my nephew, and my own head above the turbulent waters. I am fucked. I can't even let myself dwell on all the ways of screwed I am right now, because that bitch is going down.

I make quick work of cleaning out my locker, grabbing my stuff, and telling Brenda, the manager, that I will call her to discuss Dr. Shannon's behavior. She feels terrible, but we both know it would be pointless to continue to fight with him.

When I push through the lobby doors into the parking lot and see Mandy frantically stabbing my tires with a knife, I lose it. In hindsight, it might not have been the smartest move to charge a woman with a large knife, but fucking hell, I am done with this.

"You crazy little shit!" I yell, watching her eyes go all wonky. Throwing my box on the ground, I make quick work of the distance between us, bend at the waist, and knock her ass to the ground. My mind doesn't register the sharp pain in my arm long enough for me to even give it a thought. Taking her hand with the knife, I slam it into the ground and watch her eyes widen and water with the pain. She lets her grip slacken, and I quickly throw the knife away with my other hand.

"You stupid, pathetic, little shit! Not sure what you think you had with Greg, but he is done. You want me to think you're someone special to him, but sweetheart, you forget that he has already made it clear he is done with you."

"He is mine," she growls. "You will never have him!"

"Oh, that is where you're wrong. I already have him." I smile sweetly at her, but when her face contorts into what I can only describe as wacked to the highest power, I know she is past seeing reason.

"Really? Well he was in *my* bed last night, and every night before that! He might have fun with you, but he always comes home to me."

"You're insane." I move to get off her, and then she pounces, grabbing a hold of my hair and slamming me down to the ground. My head knocks on the asphalt for a second, but not long enough to keep me from shaking it off and springing back.

Not even concerned with the hold she has on my hair, I rear back and slam my fist into her gut. Her grip loosens instantly. I follow that with one more to her temple and watch her eyes go hazy before she falls to the ground.

"Oh my God! Melissa! Melissa! Are you okay, sweetie?" I turn around and watch Brenda running out of the office door with the phone pressed to her ear, "I called the police, saw the whole thing, oh my God! Oh my GOD!"

"I'm okay Brenda, promise. Give me a minute, okay?" I walk over and place the one call that to me is more important than calling the police right now. Greg. Not only is this his mess but I can't deny I would feel better with him here.

After the quick call to him that has my blood pressure jumping again, I hang up and can't hold back the smile that takes over my face.

Yeah, I want him here, and not because of the mess, which arguably is his fault, but I want him here because he makes me happy. And for the first time, in a long time I am embracing that happiness without the fear that something will take it away from me.

The police came and took Brenda's statements and mine. Since 'Barbie' is still passed out in front of my car, they call the ambulance to take her to the hospital. Luckily, the parking lot is monitored so they tell me they will collect the security footage and get back to me if they have any further questions. Brenda is shocked when I tell them I'm not pressing charges. That is my own deal and I'm not changing my mind. She wants to start more shit, let her; I'll be waiting next time.

Unlucky for me, Greg shows up when the paramedic is cleaning the graze on my arm from my run in with the knife. Nothing bad, but there's enough blood covering my arm and scrub top that he takes one look at me and goes solid. I'm talking you can feel his fury hit hard.

He make it to me in two large steps, takes in my face and his eyes roams every inch of my body making sure there isn't anything he is missing.

"You didn't tell me she hurt you. You didn't tell me that she attacked you." He didn't seem mad at me but still, I decide it will be best to lead with caution here.

"I think that it might be a correct assessment of the situation if you were to say that I, technically, attacked her." His eyes that have been looking at the white bandage against my skin shoot up to mine and I can't miss the humor that flashes briefly before concern takes over again.

"I'm sorry?" he questions.

"Well, one thing you might want to know about me is that I won't lay down and let someone fuck my life. She was messing with my car and in turn, fucking me. This happened ten minutes after she got me fired from my job and threw so much garbage around the office that I doubt I will find work for years. So, yes... it's safe to say I attacked her."

"Okay. Not sure I know what to do with *that,* but we can come back to that later. Are you okay?"

"Greg, I'm fine. I just caught the knife for a second but it's nothing but a flesh wound." I smile at his handsome face and try to ease some of the anger I can still feel coming off of him in waves. "If it makes you feel better, she looks a lot worse."

He holds my eyes for a few minutes before he lets out a deep laugh. "Not wild about seeing you hurt, Beauty. Are you done here? What do you say we head back to my place and you can fill me in on the rest of the stuff you just said, yeah?"

"Yeah, Greg, that sounds good."

Brenda hands me my box that until that moment, I had completely forgotten about, and after we wait for the tow truck to take my junker away, we head off to his house. On the way over, I make a call to my mom letting her know that I had some car trouble and I would be over tomorrow.

I know my problems will still be waiting for me in the morning but right now, I need this. I need Greg. Shockingly, the thought of needing someone else doesn't terrify me.

CHAPTER 17
Greg

After her quick call, she puts her phone away and is asleep in seconds. It isn't long after that when her head hits my shoulder and her arms curl around my arm. Hell, she can pull the damn limb off if it makes her feel better.

When I pulled up at the pediatrician's office and saw her sitting on the curb *bleeding,* I almost lost my damn mind. I'm no stranger to the feeling of overwhelming protectiveness. But I have never felt it this powerfully. Never has every inch of my body turned to stone-cold fury in seconds. There is no doubt in my mind after that; she is mine. And judging by how quickly her body turned to mine in her sleep, she knows this too. Her mind just hasn't caught up with her heart and body.

I wave at Stan as we drive through the gate. Taking the long ride through the neighborhood gives me a few extra minutes with her resting against my body. It gives me time to enjoy her unguarded trust a little longer.

When we pull up at my house, she still doesn't stir. I turn off the truck and unfold my body before making my way to her side. I stand there for a few minutes just taking her all in. Running my fingers lightly across the bandage on her arm brings it all home, and the vice on my heart gives a tight squeeze. I caused this. Maybe not directly, but in my mind, it's the same thing and it is killing me.

"Beauty," I murmur, stroking her hair lightly. Her eyes flutter a few times before meeting mine. "Come on, let's get inside, and lay down?" It's early, not even close to dinnertime, but if laying down makes her feel better, safer, then that's fine with me.

"I'm okay; just needed a little power snooze." Her voice is husky with sleep, causing me to fight with myself to keep my lust at bay.

"Alright, well let's get settled and you can fill me in on the details, yeah?"

"Sure thing, baby." I know she just woke up, and most likely doesn't even realize she said that, but that word goes straight to my heart. Zaps right through and causes it to fill with so much elation. I should be worried; after all, the woman has the power to level my world.

We make our way inside and settle. Sitting down on the couch, I don't even give her time to consider sitting somewhere else in the room, I grab her hand and pull her onto my lap. My arms enclose around her and I let out a low, relieved breath.

"Fill me in, babe?"

She looks into my eyes for a few minutes, for what I'm not sure, but she must have found it because she begins her story. Not easy to hear, but damn I'm proud of her for sticking up for herself. When she stops talking, I can't even speak. I have to keep myself still to control the fury and the need to do *something*.

"You didn't press charges? Please tell me, Melissa, that I heard you wrong there?" She looks up into my eyes, slightly confused at my tone. "Not angry with you baby. Just trying to figure out why you wouldn't press charges against her."

"I just want her gone. I don't know her, and I know you and her had your thing, but this is a little too much."

The hand that has been lightly stroking her thigh stills. "And you're going to let this shit come between us?"

"I didn't say that. What I said was it's too much. I lost my job because of her, Greg. My job and my family's income, all gone because of your fuck buddy."

"Baby, I get that this is some heavy shit but you need to understand that I wasn't a saint before I met you. I wasn't perfect, not even close, but that shit with Mandy ended when we started. Not that there was much to end, but I made it clear to her at the wedding that we were finished. I made it clear again, when she showed up at the gate throwing more shit. I don't know what's going on in her mind but I'll find out. I don't want you to worry about her."

"I believe you. I do, but that doesn't change the fact that I lost a lot more today than just some skin on my arm." I flinch at the reminder of just how dangerous this situation was today.

"Let me take care of it, baby."

"How are you going to take care of this?" Her brow furrows, and confusion mixed with disbelief flashes in her eyes.

"First, you're going to let me deal with Mandy but I still want a restraining order on her. Second, I know some people around town. I just did a security install for a general practitioners office right down the street. Just let me call and see if he's hiring. Third, let me in. Just let me in, Beauty.

The silence around us while she takes in my words is heavy. She doesn't want to let me in. I know this, but that doesn't mean that I will stop until she at least lets me have the chance to prove to her I deserve it.

"Meli, baby," I sigh. "Trust me when I tell you that I have lived a life that makes me know when something is worth fighting for. I took one look at you and knew you were worth it to me. It's new, I get that, but I know you feel it too."

"I feel it," she whispers. "I feel it and it terrifies me."

"Why? What has you scared, baby? Tell me so I can help."

"You don't understand. When I lost Fia, something inside me changed. I have always been the guarded one in the family. Mom is amazing but she is weak. Fia was the same way. They let men walk all over them and I always said I wouldn't be like that. I wouldn't need a man. My dad, piece of shit. What I do remember isn't pretty and I watched my sister relive that nightmare with no hopes of helping her. For years, I have had fun but never let a man in. Greg, you have the power to not only get in but to destroy me if you ever want back out."

"I can't make you promises, Beauty. I can't sit here and tell you that I'm worth letting those walls down for. But, I can tell you that if the way I feel for you now keeps growing, there isn't an army strong enough to pull me out. Spent too long wanting someone worth it and as crazy as it sounds? One look baby… it took one look that even being covered in Nate's vomit couldn't dim how bright that beauty knocked me down."

She laughs softly but still looks at me as if she is worried I might vanish with her next breath. "I want to be there. There's just so much going on. Now this, us, and everything else that's flying around out of control. I don't know how to just let go."

"Let me in," I stress again.

"I—I don't know how." It's like watching a caged animal try to escape. I can tell she wants to, she wants to let me in so bad, but she really doesn't know how.

"You don't have to be strong all the time. Let me take it, Beauty. Let me be your rock. Let ME fight. For Christ sake, let me be who you need."

Each word out of my mouth has her eyes widening. Hell, I don't even know where that all came from but I need her to understand. I need her to get on the same page as I am before I am the one losing myself in someone who doesn't want me.

"My mom has custody of Cohen, Fia's son, but that is only because with all the hours I work it isn't possible for me to have him. I spend as much time as I can with him, but that still isn't enough. Mom's old but can still get around. She doesn't work, because, well…she's old. And even though she can get around, that doesn't mean she does it without difficulties. My check pays for everything, which is why I live in a shit-hole apartment in the middle of the hood. Cohen and his wellbeing get it all. Do *not* think that is a complaint. I would give everything for that kid." She pauses and looks into my eyes for a few seconds before looking back at my hand resting on her leg. I give her a light squeeze and she continues, "Simon, Fia's ex, was a real douche. Already told you about him, but even though he is gone, I still feel like he is fucking with my family. His mom, Susan, has been coming around for the last year trying to get Cohen. She tried to go the legal route, but there was no judge in the world that would give her custody or even visiting rights. Bad, the worst kind of human being."

I am well informed about Susan Wagner. But I'm not letting her know about that right now. She is just letting me in, starting to let her walls down and trust me. No way am I messing with that right now.

"So, anyway. She's been causing some drama. Calling, sending letters, and coming around. She's harmless but annoying, and it scares Cohen. That is what I've been dealing with since Sunday. Trying to keep my mom calm and Cohen clueless."

"You think she will be trouble?" I question.

"No. I mean, yes for now, but I think she just misses her son, or I should say the idea of her son. She doesn't want Cohen; she just doesn't want *us* to have him."

"Seems reasonable baby, but I don't like you dealing with that alone."

"I'm not alone," she says with small smile tips up her lips.

"No, Beauty…you definitely are not."

We have been sitting here for a while just silently taking each other in when her voice breaks the stillness. "Tell me about Grace."

"Trying to change the subject?" I laugh but I really am just happy she wants to know more about me.

"I just want to know you, all of you, even that beast you only seem to throw around toward me." She smiles and leans her head on my shoulder.

"Grace was amazing. We were best friends and each other's shadow our whole lives. She didn't take it well when I enlisted but she knew it was what I wanted. Our dad was a career Marine and I knew before I could walk that that's what I would do. He was the bravest man we knew until we lost him. She knew what it meant to carry on his memory. We talked as often as we could but that still wasn't enough. I met her boyfriend once when I was home on leave and didn't like the bastard. Told her, but she was in love so there wasn't anything I could say. That was the only time we disagreed about anything. She married him shortly after I left. Twenty years old and ready to follow him around the world if he asked." I take a deep breath and think back to her beautiful smile and her violet eyes. "You would have loved her. She was a lot like Dee, always happy. You know how I got the call.

Needless to say, I didn't take that shit well. I went off the deep end. The second I could get out, I left the Marines and the only dream I've ever had behind and disappeared. Axel and the boys, hell my own mother, no one knew where I was for almost two years. Met a guy on the road who helped me sort my shit, came back home, and started my own company. The rest, as they say, is history."

"It gets better? Losing the other part of you?" She asks. I know what she means. Grace was the other part of my soul and I'm guessing her sister was hers.

"Yeah baby, it gets better. Never easy, but it gets better."

"That's good. I don't want to hurt anymore," she whispers.

"With me around, I'll do my best to make sure you never do." She pulls her head off my shoulder, shifts lightly, and brings her hands up to cup my face before dropping her forehead against mine.

"You're a good man, Greg Cage. You give me some time, and I might just fall in love with you."

"That's the plan, Beauty." I whisper and take her lips, delivering the message that I hope shows her how much I want to be worthy that love.

CHAPTER 18
Greg

When I pull Melissa off the couch and lead her upstairs to my room, I know this will be more than just burning up the sheets. This is about communicating without words what needs to be shown and not said, giving her what she needs from me, and making sure she feels 'it'. I'm no blushing virgin but even I am feeling the pressure to make sure this is something for the record books.

When we reach my bedroom, I pull her close and drop my lips to hers. Simple and slow, I make love to her mouth.

This is a slow mating. We stand there with our arms wrapped around each other and just savor. Neither of us is in a hurry, but both of us are in need. Slowly we take turns peeling the clothes from each other's bodies, and when we are both naked, we just stand there taking each other in. Her skin is flawless, glowing with a natural tan. Her tits make my mouth water and my dick jump. Those legs, my balls tighten just taking in her long legs. I knew the backside is just as good as the front; she is pure perfection and beauty.

"You going to keep devouring me with your eyes, baby?" There it is again, and this time she is wide awake.

Baby.

Reaching out and hooking her around the waist earns me a breathy sigh and I smile down at her before returning my lips to hers. Still taking my time, I enjoy the slow kiss full of desire.

My hands that rest right above her ass make the slow journey down until I have both of her globes in my hands. With a squeeze, I lift her up and am instantly rewarded when her legs wrap around my hips. My dick jumps at the contact with her wet heat.

I offer her no words as I start walking toward the bed, continuing my assault on her mouth. She is clamped so tight to my body that there wasn't room for air between us. My body feels like it is moving on autopilot. I don't need my mind to tell my body what to do. I crave her, so this is like second nature. We have only been apart two damn days and it seems like a year.

Laying her down softly, I make the move to detach my lips from hers but she tightens her arms and legs, and the soft moan she lets out is a straight shot to my dick. It's throbbing and begging me to thrust home, but this needs to be about her.

When I am finally able to release her mouth, she looks up at me and I can see the lust shining bright, but behind that, I swear I almost see adoration. I don't doubt that is what's reflecting in my own, but I never thought I would see it so soon in my Beauty's gaze.

"So beautiful," I whisper, trailing my fingers down the side of her face, her neck, and her shoulders. My eyes follow my hand as it moves over her skin. Leaning my weight onto my side, I trail my hand down to her breast. Her pink nipple puckers and strains for my mouth, but I just roam my fingers over the soft skin. Her breathing comes in sharp pants, her skin prickles with goose bumps, and when I take her nipple between my fingers, giving it a soft tug and pinch, she arches off the bed and her quick intake of air echoes in the room.

My dick might be in serious danger of early detonation if I don't hurry things along, but I can't seem to move away from her. She is just looking at me, eyes wide, and so close to that lost look she gets right before she soars.

Shifting down slightly, I take the other nipple in my mouth, swirling my tongue and hollowing my cheeks when I suck hard. She taste delicious; every part of her skin is mouthwatering.

I move my hand down her body until I meet the bare, wet skin of her pussy. A ragged groan of my own crawls up my throat when I feel just how ready she is, and I push my rock hard dick into her thigh, trying to ease some of the pressure.

"Fuck, my girl is ready for me." I say against her breast, "Always ready for me."

She hums something unidentifiable before grabbing the back of my neck and pushing her tit back to my mouth. I laugh softly against her skin before wrapping my lips around her tight bud and sucking deep, giving her everything she wants. This time I hold nothing back. My teeth nibble, my tongue licks and swirls, and when I close my lips around the tight bud and pull she screams out.

164

"So good, baby," she moans.

I switch to her other side and give her some more attention causing her hand in my hair to tighten. When I push two fingers deep inside her, she clamps down with a hold that's so fierce that I can barely move my fingers back out. Rubbing her clit with my thumb and hooking my fingers while pumping softly makes her moaning cry louder. She pulls my head back and with one look I know she's ready. My girl wants me and she isn't afraid to let me know.

"Not yet," I whisper, pulling myself up to meet her lips. I devour her, pouring myself into her with every mating of our tongue and thrust of my fingers. When I hit that spot inside that never fails to set her off, she pulls off my mouth and screams my name so loud, I'm shocked the windows didn't shatter.

I wait for her to come back down and give me her lazy eyes before I pull out and slowly lick my fingers clean, watching her eyes widen and her lips tip up slightly.

Rolling off the bed, I walk over to the other side and grab a few condoms out of the side table, the whole time her eyes never leaving me. Or I should say, they never leave my dick, which I am sure at this point has turned purple. When I walk back to the other side and stand between her parted legs, her eyes still haven't left my straining erection. I throw all but one condom on the bed and take my dick in my hand. Her eyes flash as she watches me work myself, but when her pink tongue darts out and licks her lips, I have no doubt that I am two seconds away from shooting all over her flat stomach.

Tearing open the condom, I make quick work of sheathing myself. For the first time in my life, I wish I could take her without the barrier. I understand her concerns, which is why I went to the clinic the first chance I had on Monday. Luckily, the doctor is an old friend of mine, and he promised results by the end of the week. Thank Christ; I couldn't wait to take my woman bare.

"Slide back some, baby. We will get creative later, but right now I want to be able to watch your eyes when I take you." She doesn't waste anytime moving back until her head is almost hanging off the edge. Never once closing her legs, her eyes no longer follow my dick. They are blazing up at me, begging me to hurry.

I climb up and kneel between her legs, enjoying the look of her giving herself to me with no hesitation. Her eyes never leave mine as I lean forward and steady my weight over her body. Taking my dick in my hand and rubbing her wet center, a sharp gasp rewards me every time my ring hits her clit. Best damn bet I ever took was getting my dick pierced. She loves it, and she isn't shy about letting me know with each gasp or moan that leaves her body. I can't wait for her to feel it without the latex being between us.

I lean down and brace myself with one arm by her ribs, keeping my knees apart and my dick pressed against her heat. Kissing her stomach before peppering more along the way to her neck, I slowly reach her ear. Biting it softly, I hum my approval when she moves her hips up trying to impale herself on my dick. I lean up and hold her eyes while I push just a few inches into her. She melts, no other word for it, she simples melts into the bed at the same time pushing off with her feet to try and speed up my entrance.

"Patience, baby. Feel it." No way that this connection between us can be missed. It's no wonder I was a goner for her the second we locked eyes. She feels it and there is no doubt about it when I thrust painfully slow into her body. Her eyes widen with each inch and my hips settle against hers. Her legs hook around my back, her heels digging in. Her hands snake around my back and nails bite the skin when I shift my hips and my base piercing rubs her clit.

I lean forward and kiss her deeply before pulling back and resting my forehead against hers. Only then do I begin to slowly pull out until I almost lose her heat. When I push back in just as slowly, she tries to dig in again, begging me to speed up. "Patience baby, let me love you." Her eyes widen and a sob catches in her throat. "Just let me show you. Feel it, Beauty."

Melissa

Oh my God. Did he just say that? I can't even panic completely because he's right. There isn't anything about this that doesn't scream love. His gaze is blinding with it, his touch and the way he worships my body are testaments to the fact that this is nothing but pure lovemaking. It should terrify me, I should be running, but I can't. Even though it seems rash, there isn't a way possible to detangle myself from this man, physically or mentally. He's right; I feel it. Right or wrong, regardless of how terrified I am, I will regret for the rest of my life if I don't explore this.

"I feel it baby," I reply breathlessly.

He seems shocked at first that I am voicing my agreement. His smile, so wide his eyes crinkle, hits his face and his hips make their way back down before he speaks, "Yeah, baby, feels like a dream, but so good I don't ever want to wake up."

Oh, God.

I have no willpower to resist him when he opens himself up like this.

We continue to look into each other's eyes. Our lips are inches apart and our breath dances with each exhale. My fingers clench in the thick muscles along his back and my legs hold him tightly to me. When he hits my spot again, I know it will only be seconds before I lose it. I can feel my release already forming, growing, and slowly spreading through my body like a warm blanket. Ribbons of pleasure unfold from my belly, tingles dance up my spine, and my skin heats to the point of pain.

"So… close, so close," I moan against his lips. He pulls forward again and rolls his hips, forcing the barbell to rub against my swollen clit. My release hits with such powerful force that I scream, claw at his back, and grind myself against him like a hussy. Jesus, this man does things to my body that I have never felt.

He keeps moving slowly as my arched back falls back down on to the bed, just watching me with his burning eyes.

"Yeah. You feel it, baby." He says in a voice so rife with strain that I know he is working hard to keep his control. "Amazing."

He drops his head to my shoulder and rests it there for a few seconds while he continues his slow rhythmic assault. I rub my hands up and down his back, enjoying the soft growls that vibrate against my chest.

"Look at us, baby." His request seems odd until he lifts his head off my shoulder and repeats himself. "Look at us. Watch me love you."

Following his gaze down to where our bodies join, my eyes take in his thick length as it stretches my body to receive him. His dick is soaked with my release, and every time he disappears deep into my body, his piecing caresses my clit. We both watch for a few minutes, but when the pleasure becomes too much, my head presses against the bed as my eyes roll back, and I clamp down on him again. Screaming his name out into the expanse of his room and listening to it bounce off the walls, my sounds mingle with his own cry of release.

We lay there trying to come back down for what felt like hours. Our combined sweat covering my skin begins to dry, leaving me chilled where his body isn't covering mine. We don't speak, but words aren't needed. I feel it and he isn't wrong about that. Not only was that the most powerful sex I have ever experienced, but he wasn't wrong when he said that he was going to love me. I might already be halfway there myself.

He rolls to the side, taking my cheek in his big hand and turns my head to meet his gaze. "Whatever this might have been for you before now baby, there is no trying or going slow. I know you felt it; it was all over your face. I feel like I just found a piece of myself that has been lost forever. A piece of the puzzle that I didn't even know was missing until you walked into my life. This, us… baby, I will work as hard as I can and then some to prove to you that you have nothing to fear."

He catches the tear that leaks from my eye with his lips, and follows that up with a kiss to my lips before leaving the bed and walking into the bathroom. I hear the shower turn on and a few seconds later, he returns, scoops me off the bed, and carries me into the warm spray. After cleaning every inch of my skin and then his own, he shows me again what it feels like to be loved.

When we finally fall back into the bed, he curls me tight into his body, and with his strong arms holding me close, I surrender to sleep. The last thought that filters through my mind before I fade off is that I don't feel so scared anymore if this is what love feels like.

CHAPTER 19
Melissa

It's been a little over a month since Greg and I officially became an 'us'. It hasn't been perfect, but it's been damn near close. True to his word, a few days after Dr. Shannon fired me, Greg set up an interview with Dr. Roberts. He is an older family man who runs his own practice. Over the years, he has added more doctors to his team, and now, he has the need for more nursing staff. He is one of those people you love to work for and lucky for me, he wanted me on his team. I started the week after I was fired and am the happiest I have ever been at work. It also helps that my pay jumped a lot. There are no more struggles, no more worrying about how I am going to stretch my check to make sure that we're all comfortable.

I have talked to Greg about helping me find a new apartment since I can now afford rent in a nicer, safer complex. This is what started our first real fight. He doesn't see the need in my paying to live somewhere when I spend all my time at his place anyway. This, coincidently, is because he took one look at my apartment and the neighborhood I lived in the day after we became us, turned right around without parking, and refused to take me back. I get where he is coming from and to be honest, I have never felt safe there anyway. So if he wants to act like a grown toddler and keep me hostage, who am I to complain? It comes with one kickass house and the best sex ever.

And to be completely honest, I don't want to be away from him.

I still have my apartment, but the majority of my stuff has slowly started to make its way to his house. Some of it because I need it, but I'm starting to wonder if he is pocketing my belongings and then moving them to his house when I'm not looking. Either way, we are pretty much living together at this point.

Our second fight was over my car. Even though it was ready a few days after Mandy pulled her crazy on it, Greg, without letting me know, told the mechanic to sell it. The next day a brand new Honda sat in the driveway of his house. We fought about it for a good day. He had to endure my silence, but when he finally had enough, he calmly told me that he wanted me safe. My old car couldn't offer that so he took care of it. When that didn't work, he pulled me close and said, "Baby, after I lost Grace in a car accident, do you think you could please just give a little here? I want to know you are safe when I can't be with you." Yeah, call me whipped but that is all it took.

We have done all the traditional couple things. We date, we go out with friends, he met my mom, and we have tons and tons of sex. I am starting to believe that Greg Cage is unbelievably close to perfection.

Things with Susan have also calmed down over the weeks. She's called a few times but usually only when she is drunk out of her mind. Mom and I think she will eventually forget that Cohen exists and just leave us alone.

One thing we don't have to worry about is Mandy. That is another promise that Greg kept. The next day, he drove me to the police station and helped me fill out the necessary reports to have a restraining order against her. Although he assures me that it won't ever be needed, he still feels better knowing it's there. He didn't tell me until later that week that he had a 'come to Jesus' (as my mom calls it) with Mandy. I don't care what happens to the bitch, but according to him, she is back on her meds and seeking help. 'Back on the meds' should have been clue enough that she really is a psycho bitch. Maybe next time, she will keep up with those damn pills. All that matters is he says that she won't be a problem, and I believe him.

About two weeks ago, I started to bring Cohen around. If there was any doubt left in my mind that Greg was the perfect man, watching him with my nephew squashed it. It is clear that he is meant to have children in his life but when he started asking me about my plans for the future when it came to Cohen, I start to worry a little that maybe kids aren't something he wants. I can't help my fears; it all just seems so perfect that I keep waiting for 'it' to happen and all of this to just blow up in my face.

So, I told him the truth. I wanted Cohen. My mom wants me to have Cohen. He is a crazy-as-hell three-year-old boy who needs someone that can keep up with him. He smiled and told me that was a great plan, and then continued to sit there with me for hours and plan *our* future with Cohen in it.

That was also the night that I realized I had fallen in love with him.

We are closing in on autumn and the weather is still nice enough to enjoy being outside for long periods. So here I am, in Greg's kitchen, making lunch for the two most important men in my life. Greg and Cohen are spending some time doing what Cohen calls 'man fluff, no hips', which, when translated by a hysterical Greg, means 'man stuff babe, no chicks allowed.' They left a few hours ago to do whatever it is that boys do. My mom has graciously taken me up on my offer to start having Cohen spend some weekends with me. Now that I have somewhere I feel safe enough to take him, we are finally spending some quality time together.

I have just cut up the last sandwich when I hear the front door open and little feet pound down the hall.

"Melwee! Melwee, look what I got!" And like a flash, in comes Cohen with a bright red cape flapping behind him. "Greg said this would help me fight ninjas. He said that all ninjas are scared of superheroes. He said that if I have a cape I have MAGIC! Magic powers that ninjas can't fight because they aren't SUPERheroes! Melwee! Do you see? Can you see it?" The whole time he is giving this speech, he doesn't once take a breath. By the time he's finished, he has to take a few deep ones just to stay on his feet. I look over and see Greg leaning against the doorframe, his arms crossed over his thick chest and a huge grin on his face. I give him one of my own before turning my attention back to Cohen, who is now spinning in circles and kicking his feet out every few seconds. My guess, he's fighting ninjas now and completely forgotten about us.

"Come here and let me see your powers, little man. I can already tell that the ninjas are going to be so scared of you! I bet they don't even come near Nana's house anymore!"

He stops his weird twirl kicking and jumps into my arms. "Can you feel my power?" he whispers loudly into my face. "Greg said that I have powers against you too," he says still whispering loudly.

"Oh he does, does he?" I ask and look over at Greg, watching as his silent laughter shakes his body.

"Co, my man, not something you're supposed to tell the ladies." Greg laughs in response to Cohen and walks over to ruffles his hair.

"Alright, tell me, little guy, what kind of powers do you have against me?"

"I can make you love me!" He laughs and looks over at Greg nodding his little head, "Greg said that I can make you love me and all I have to do is smile! He told me it worked on him, so it has to be magic powers, Melwee! He told me. He said all I have to do is smile and everyone falls in love with me because I'm special like that."

Well. Shit. My throat has closed up now and I can feel my eyes prickling. I am going to cry. "He did?" I croak.

"Melwee, what's wrong with your face? You look funny. Like that time you dropped something on your foot and yelled that *really* bad word; your face looks like that." He takes both my cheeks in his small hands and moves my head around, studying every inch. "Yeah, you look funny." Then he wiggles to get down and takes off running through the house, yelling for the ninjas to watch out because he's going to hunt them down.

"You should probably go make sure he doesn't destroy the house," I whisper to Greg, who is now pulling me into his arms.

"Don't care about anything in the house he can break."

"Not even your brand new flat screen?" I question, still trying to control my emotions.

"Nope."

"Not even that really expensive computer?"

"Not even that."

"You love him?" He bends slightly and places a kiss on my nose. When he pulls back, I can see it. His smile is huge, all the way to his eyes, making his laugh lines deepen. Those blue eyes I love so much are sparkling with humor, but clear as day, I can see it.

"Yeah, Beauty, I love him."

"Oh." Pathetic but that's all I have for him. I am sure my 'funny face' just got funnier. I can't stop the tears if I try. The thought of this man, who has already stolen my heart, loving Cohen as much as I do, is just too much to hold in.

"Babe, how can you can be so blind when your eyes are wide open? Even if he wasn't the coolest kid I have ever met, even if I didn't enjoy the hell out of my time reliving my childhood with the little guy, he is part of you. No, he isn't yours and I understand that, but he is part of *you,* and Beauty, how can I not love that?"

Oh. God.

"Oh," I repeat and crash my head into his chest. He laughs a few times before cupping my face and lightly pulling my head off his chest.

"Oh? That's all you got for me?" He jokes. How he can joke right now is beyond me.

"What do you want me to say? You need to be clear with me, baby, because I don't want to misinterpret something you could be saying right now." My voice sounds funny and the tears have already started falling freely. He just keeps smiling down at me, both of his warm palms against my neck and his thumbs keep sweeping away my tears. All the while, he just keeps smiling.

"Alright. I love having you in my house, going to sleep with your body pressed close to mine and waking up with you still in my arms. I love coming home and having dinner with you in my house, watching movies on the couch with you laying on top of me. I love getting your calls every time something ridiculous happens that you just can't wait to tell me about. I love Cohen. He's amazing, and one day I would love to be a permanent part of his life.

But, I don't love him because he's great. No, I want to be a permanent fixture in his life because I am deeply in love with his aunt. Beauty, I love you."

"You love me?" I whisper again after a few moments of just taking him in.

"Yeah, I do. Completely." His strong voice wraps around me and his love is like a blanket of warmth. I can feel it like a tangible thing taking over the room.

"I love you too. God, I do… so much." My silent tears have turned into sobs now. He lets my face go for a second, but only to pick me up by my hips and sit me down on the countertop. My legs open automatically, and he steps in, arms going around my body as he tucks my head into his neck.

"Baby, best I can see, this is a good thing. Why are you crying about it?" he asks, his voice rumbling against my ear. He stands there with my head against his chest and lets me have my moment. Silently being my rock, my strength, and just lets me have this.

When I hear some loud bangs and Cohen's battle cry of victory, I know it's only a matter of time before our moment is interrupted. I pull back and wipe my eyes before looking into Greg's eyes.

"You love me?" I ask again, but this time letting my happiness show, and I smile so big, it even hurts a little.

He throws his head back and his laughter rings out around us. "Yeah, I do."

"That's good."

"You're wrong, babe," he says with a smile. "It's not good, it's fucking amazing."

Since it is Sunday and Greg and I both start work pretty early, we bring Cohen home before dinner so that we can go out and have some us time before the week starts. This is also something we try to do during the week. When things get crazy at the Corp Security offices, it is sometimes past dinner when he gets home. So if we have time, we make it a point to spend special time like this together.

'Super Co', which is what we have been instructed to call Cohen now, takes off into my mom's house the second Greg parks. His cape flaps in the wind behind him, and we can already hear him starting his speech with my mom. Greg walks over and takes my hand before we head into the house.

When we make it to the kitchen, Cohen is still screaming about all his magic. "Oh my, that is some good news, baby." My mom smiles at us and gives Cohen a big kiss before he runs off to his room to make sure there aren't any ninjas.

"That boy is so funny sometimes," she says shaking her head. "Meli-Kate, come here baby." I let Greg go and walk into her arms. "You look happy today," she whispers in my ear.

"I am," I whisper back. "I really am."

"That's good, baby. You deserve that." She pulls back and gives me a kiss on my forehead before turning to my man.

"Come here handsome and give this old lady some thrills." And here starts my mother's weekly enjoyment in my boyfriend and embarrassing me at every turn.

"Lilly," he says and walks up, wraps his arms around her, and lifts her off her feet in a big hug.

She laughs loud and slaps him playfully on the arm when he lets her down. "Such a strong man! Take my girl home and show her a good night." She giggles and I turn beat red.

"Mom! Jesus!" They both laugh, enjoying this new tag team effort to embarrass me.

We stay in the kitchen for a while before Greg excuses himself to go say goodbye to Cohen. How did I miss how much he cares for my nephew for so long?

I don't realize that I have been looking at the empty hallway in a daze until my mother's soft laughter curls around me. "Oh, my darling girl, you have it bad."

I look over and smile at my mother. Her eyes are misting with emotion but sadness isn't one of them. Her smile is huge and you can tell she is happy for me to have found this. "You have no idea just how bad I have it. He's incredible mom and he loves Cohen. Can you believe it?

He loves that crazy kid just as if he were his own. Just like we do."

"I know that, baby. Could've saved you the trouble of figuring out all this on your own but I knew you would get there. He's a keeper, Meli-Kate. I know I don't have the best record when it comes to judging men. First with your father and then... well, I just don't. But, with a man like that, there is no doubt. He is the kind of man you dream of baby. Don't ever let your past cloud that knowledge."

"I won't. I love you, mama."

"I know that, sweetheart." We give each other a hug and sit down to chat about things happening this week while we wait for the boys to do their thing. About thirty minutes or so later, Greg comes walking back in laughing.

"He was just mid-sentence and fell asleep. We were sitting there talking about the best ways to take out flying ninjas and bam, his little head just face planted into my lap and he was out. Lilly, I went ahead and changed him into pajamas so you wouldn't have to bother with that."

She smiles brightly at him, leans in, and whispers in my ear, "Keeper."

Not long after that, we leave and head downtown to our favorite burger joint. We have just sat down when his phone rang and he excuses himself to take the call outside. He has only been gone a few minutes when he comes back inside looking agitated.

"You okay?"

"Yeah, I'm okay. Just some shit from Axel but no big deal. Look, I ran into Mandy outside. Nothing happened, but let's get out of here, okay?"

Damn. Just when you think that woman is gone for good. "Sure, baby."

We pay the bill and get our meals boxed up. On the way out, I see Mandy standing next to a few girlfriends. Doesn't bother me to see her, but what does bother me is the look she gives me. She might fool others, but I can see the pure evil behind that carefully crafted mask. And I just know she isn't done with us.

That night, after three mind-blowing orgasms, I lay wrapped in Greg's arms and asked him about his call with Axel. I had forgotten that when he mentioned Mandy that he looked upset, more upset that he normally is when seeing her face. I don't like knowing he is bothered with anything if there is a chance I can help it.

"Baby?" I question, lifting my head off his chest.

"Hmm," he responds, still running his fingers across my back. His eyes are closed and his face is blank but peaceful.

"What did Axel want tonight?"

His eyes snap open, and a look that I don't like at all replaces his blank expression. He's hiding something and doing a shit job at it. "Nothing Beauty. Just some shit we have been discussing for a while now."

I could press, and my gut is telling me I should, but my pride is stopping me. I know him, and whatever is bothering him is cutting him deep. He'll tell me when he's ready, but I hate thinking there is a secret between us.

"Okay. If you want to talk, just let me know."

His eyes flash but whatever it is that was there is gone before I can figure it out, "I know. Love you, Beauty."

"Love you too."

For the first time in weeks, my sleep isn't peaceful.

CHAPTER 20
Greg

I have been lying in bed with Melissa draped across my body for the last two hours, unable to fall asleep. Today had been a perfect day, but when Axel called, and two seconds into the conversation asked me if I had told her yet, my mood quickly went to shit. When we weren't doing this back and forth debate over why it was so important that I do it right now. It turned heated before I could stop it.

I know he is right. I need to tell Melissa my connection with Simon Wagner. And I needed to do it yesterday. The more time that goes by, the more the ball of worry grows in my gut. I don't think she would have taken it so bad if I told her sooner, but now that we are both solidly invested in this relationship and our feelings are finally put out there, well... I don't think this is going to go well.

Turning around after biting out, "I'll fucking tell her about Simon tomorrow; just shut the fuck up about it," and seeing Mandy standing behind me is not a welcome site. There's no telling how long she has been there but any amount of time is too long. I have stupidly just let it all out and if she has been there long enough, she knows the one thing that I am keeping from my girl, the one thing that might have the power to come between us.

I don't even spare her a second of my time. I walk in, grab my girl, and get the hell out of there.

And not once since that phone call has my heart calmed down. I need to tell her and then deal with the fall out. I can tell when she questions me about Axel's call that she doesn't completely believe what I have to say. With good reason too, since she knows me well enough to know I am keeping something from her.

The next morning isn't much better. We both oversleep, so by the time we make it downstairs, we have just enough time for a quick kiss before we head to work. I follow behind her, and watch her pull off into her office before continuing down the street to Corps.

Things around here have, thankfully been quiet over the last few weeks. Luckily, the gold sidewalk seems to keep Sway in a good enough mood that he doesn't mess with us nearly as much as he used to. I did catch him sprinkling glitter on Coop a few times, and that is enough to keep us all laughing for a week, at least.

Emmy is doing better, but I can still see some pain in her eyes. She has decided it is best to distance herself completely from Maddox. I don't know if that is something she is consciously doing but he isn't happy about it.

I have just sat down to start looking over emails when my door opens and Axel walks in.

"You still have that stick up your ass?" He says and sits down in front of me.

"Fuck off."

"Oh, so I see, not only is the stick still there, but you might have just shoved that shit a little higher, huh?"

"Jesus Christ. What? What do you want me to say? No, we didn't talk last night because once I got off the phone with you, which was already interrupting our dinner, I had to walk right into motherfucking Mandy. So no, by the time I got home and loved my woman good, I wasn't in the mood to taint that shit."

He leans back and lets out a long huff. "I get you man, I do, but that shit is not going to be pretty."

"You don't think I already know this? I'm not looking forward to not only opening those old wounds, but rubbing salt in them when I tell her. You don't think I feel guilty enough? I could have stopped him, Axel! I could have stopped him, but instead of sticking around, I took off for years of booze and pussy to try and forget. I let him slip through the cracks and in turn, the man who killed my sister married hers. Oh, pretty fucking hilarious move by fate there. Throwing us together finally, only to have *that* between us."

"Seriously, G? That's what's been eating you? How in the fuck do you feel like it could even remotely be your fault that he ended up with her sister? You didn't introduce them, you didn't pull the fucking trigger, so I just don't understand how you are adding one and one and getting five." He leans forward and rests his elbows on his knees before continuing. "Brother, that isn't on you so don't hold it there."

"But it is, Axel. It is."

And that is the root of the problem. After Grace died, I was too torn up to stick around and deal with anything. My mother lost her damn mind and spent the years I disappeared slowly letting her heart wither away. By the time I had my head pulled out of my ass and got back to her, she wasn't doing well. She made it another year before I lost her too. My head wasn't in the right place to deal with Simon Wagner.

By the time I started my business in Atlanta and finally tracked him down, I was shocked to learn he was just a few counties over and had remarried. That was when I started to keep an eye on him when I could. And when I couldn't, I had Derrick. What a fucking joke.

"You need to get it done but you also need to stop blaming yourself for shit that is not your fault."

"Hear you, brother, but that doesn't mean I'm going to agree with you right now."

After a few minutes of silence, he leaves me to my silent brooding.

Melissa calls a little while later to let me know she is going to go out with Izzy and the girls for dinner tonight. Hopefully that means she will have a few glasses of wine and come home in a good mood. But, this also gives me a chance to work up my nerve to have the talk with her that I have been putting off for weeks.

"Hey, Greg," Emmy says as she walks into my office and puts some files on the desk. "Did *she* talk to you?" By the way she stresses the word 'she', I know she isn't talking about Melissa. They have become thick as thieves recently and unless I've missed a major fight, they still are.

"Uh, she would be who?" I ask.

"Seriously? God, I can't stand that woman. Mandy. She was here about an hour ago. Walked past while I was on the phone so I couldn't stop her. I think you were talking with Axel. Anyway, she was right back and out the door a few minutes later so I just assumed you had kicked her out of here."

"Fuck," I hiss. "She was here?"

"Uhmm, yes?" I can tell she looks slightly worried that I am this pissed about Mandy showing up. She has already started backing out of the office when I shake myself clear of the fury raging.

"Emmy, not upset with you. Next time you see her, do not let her past those doors. Drop the phone if you have to. Hell, throw the damn thing at her, but she doesn't make it two steps into this building, yeah?"

"Sure, okay, Greg." She furrows her brow and makes a hasty retreat out the door.

Goddammit. This is not another kink that I need in my day . Who the fuck knows what Mandy wants now, but

I know one thing, no good is going to come with finding out.

The day gets worse and then worse again as it goes on. There isn't a damn thing except Melissa's lunchtime hello call that is bright and happy about it. By the time I get home, I'm in such a shit mood and exhausted from my mind running wild all day that I crash on the couch and pass out within a few minutes of clicking on the TV. Which is unfortunate for me, since I am sleeping, I miss all of the phone calls from Izzy, then Dee and Emmy and finally Axel a few hours later.

The one call I don't miss is from Melissa. And that is because it never came.

CHAPTER 21
Melissa

Work has been typically normal. Dr. Roberts is in a good mood so it's easy to follow his lead. I am still a little worried about Greg and what is bothering him but I am determined to make today a good one. I make sure to call him a few times during the day just to make sure he's okay and each time his voice sounds more and more troubled. I hate knowing he is hurting even if it's something he is keeping from me. It still hurts to know he feels like he needs to.

When Izzy calls with the idea for an impromptu girl's night, I am all over that. I'm not avoiding going home but I'm still not eager. I get off work early and run home to change out of my scrubs before heading over to Heavy's to meet the girls. I pass Greg on the way out, but he isn't watching the other lane and doesn't see me, I consider calling but figure I won't be gone long so there isn't a need. When I get home, I will sit him down and ask him to talk to me.

I know my man, and he might not want to tell me what is hanging over his head, but if I ask, he will.

I get to Heavy's right when Dee and Izzy are pulling up. Dee bounces over with her carefree smile firmly in place.

"Hey, you! Don't you look all casual hot tonight! Izzy," she screams over her shoulder. "You see this? This is how you pull of jeans and tees!"

"Shut it, Dee! I haven't worn mine in years; you know why? Because you threw them all out! Like a deranged fashion fairy. Who does that?" She laughs at Dee. These two have the kind of friendship that anyone would be envious of. I am beyond lucky to have them in my life.

"You two are crazy, you know that? Where's Emmy?" I look around the parking lot but don't see her, or her car. "I passed Greg on the way over, so I know she isn't at the office anymore. He never leaves with her still there."

They both exchange looks, the kind of looks that communicate everything with just one glance.

"What? Did something happen?" Emmy and I are growing the kind of friendship that Izzy and Dee have. The thought that something is wrong with her hits me hard. I know she is dealing with her feelings for Maddox and after what happened at Izzy and Axel's wedding, I think we decided it is best to back off for a while. That girl, her heart is too big for her own body.

"No, nothing happened, but I know Mad is sick of her freezing him out. According to Coop, who heard it from Beck, who heard it from Sway, they had it out in the parking lot this afternoon. I don't know much after that. Axel doesn't know what happened because he took the afternoon off to keep Nate so I could get some work done. I called her and she sounded fine, but she says she wants to stay in tonight." Izzy finishes speaking and turns to walk inside.

"That's it? You just let her off the hook with some lame excuse? You guys know her; if something's happened, she's hurting."

"Meli, there isn't anything we can do. She has to realize on her own that he isn't going to come around. I told her I would stop by before I went home. She needs this time." I look at Dee as if she has lost her damn mind. The last person that should give Emmy any sort of relationship advice is Dee. Love her, but damn she is just as screwed up.

"Really, Dee? Is that the path you decided to use between you and Beck?" She flinches and I instantly regret my jab. "I'm sorry, Dee, that wasn't cool. I've got some shit on my mind and I didn't mean to take it out on you."

"It's okay. Really, I know y'all don't understand where I am with Beck because I have never told you. I just know what it's like to want the impossible, okay. Give her some time." She gives me a weak smile before turning and walking over to Izzy, who is impatiently waiting to get inside. For such a small thing, she puts away BBQ like a grown man.

We have been enjoying our dinner for a while and discussing everything that has been going on since our last get together. We try to make girls night at least once a week but because of Nate's being sick last week and Dee having to go up to North Carolina to deal with something at her other office, it has just been me and Emmy.

"What's going on up at the other branch? You seem to be doing bi-weekly trips these days." From my understanding, she has the other branch of her insurance company so fine-tuned that she could disappear for a year and it will be fine. Even Greg says that he is impressed with the crew she has running it.

She sighs deeply and looks around. "Do *not* tell the boys okay? I don't want them dealing with it until I know more. There are some inconsistencies in the books. Payments coming in on big policies but the records are all over the place and it looks like there are some funds that are missing. I'm taking care of it. I just don't want the guys going in, guns blazing, and causing more trouble than necessary."

"Um, Dee, I hate to point out the obvious but how exactly are you going to take care of this without one of them catching wind? You know they wouldn't do anything without asking first." Izzy knows them better than I do, but even I think she is full of shit. If they know that one of 'their' girls is in trouble they will move heaven and earth to fix the problem. I decide it was wiser to keep my mouth shut at this point and watch them hash this shit.

"I have it under control, Izzy. Once I figure out what's going on, I will let them know and they can help me figure out where to go from there. I don't want this made into a big deal. I could lose clients if this got out."

"Not to point out the obvious," I interrupt, "but isn't Maddox like computer geek to the stars? He could probably hack into the servers up there and figure out the trail before you even had time to fly up there. Why not let him in and get it done quick?"

"That's not a bad idea, Dee." Izzy chimes in.

"No. You know he might be all silently supportive of you Izzy, but if he knows there is trouble, he won't keep his mouth shut."

"I think you're wrong, but then again, you know them better than I do. I'm going to run to the restroom and hit up the bar for a refill; y'all want something other than beer?" I get up from the table and let them have a moment to hash it out. Izzy can get through to her better than I can.

Maybe if I hadn't been running through all the things that might be wrong with Dee and her company, or between Emmy and Maddox, or what is wrong with Greg, I might have noticed the trap I was walking straight into. I take two steps into the bathroom and there she is. Legs braced apart and arms folded over her ridiculously large tits, she has what I assume is a scowl on her Botox face.

"Jesus, what do you want? You do realize you're breaking your restraining order right?" I ignore her and continue into the stall. When I finish up, she is still standing there in the same position. Hard to tell if she is glaring at me or if her face is frozen. "What?! You really don't want to piss me off tonight Mandy, like really do not want to."

"Where is your boyfriend tonight?" God, even her voice makes me want to poke my ears with knives.

"Where my man is definitely isn't any of your business. How about you tell me what this shit is about so I can get back to enjoying my evening and get back to MY man."

"You really are a stupid bitch." She throws her head back and laughs. Sounds like an evil little troll.

I walk over to her and get close, close enough to make sure if she pisses me off, I can take care of her without too much effort. "What. Do. You. Want?" I drive each word home with small jabs into her fake tits. "Hmm, they even feel rock hard. Surely that isn't the look you paid for?"

"Shut up!" She squawks. Yes, squawks. The sound that comes out of her mouth sounds like the noise you hear when you're standing on the beach and millions of sea gulls attack. This bitch is insane.

"Mandy, I'm tired and don't want any shit right now. Can you please just get this shit moving?"

"Tell me, does Greg tell you everything? Is it complete happiness in paradise? I know how to please a man like him, and I can promise you he isn't happy. He likes it a certain way, and I doubt you have that kind of... spunk."

"Spunk? Do you know what the hell spunk is? Trust me, honey, when it comes to Greg, I get plenty of *spunk* out of it."

She looks at me confused for a few seconds, clearly confused by my comment. I had a friend in high school that had just moved to America from London and every time my mom would call her spunky, she would die. She said that to her, spunk has always meant sperm. We liked to call people spunky when they were pissing us off, because to us, being called sperm was hilarious. I don't care how old you are, that shit never gets old.

"What? Never mind. Answer me. Do you two have any secrets? I know you do, which is a shame because he never kept anything from me." My stomach drops, because even though I know she is bat shit crazy, we do have secrets. Or at least he has secrets from me. Two days ago I would have laughed in her face and maybe popped one of her tits but today, no today I already have that seed of doubt planted so deep all she did was water it and watch it grow.

"Really? Are you this demented that you need to start making up lies?" The smug smile that curls her fake features chills me to the bones.

"Went to see him today. When he saw me last night, he begged me to come to the office and talk with him. I knew it would only be a matter of time before he was sick of you, so I waited. I waited and I was right. But, I was shocked to learn just why he was done with you."

"Mandy, you are fucking nuts. I'm gone. Not going to stand here and listen to you lie about MY man.

You hear that, and get it through your fucking head; he is not yours and he never will be." I move to walk around her but she sidesteps me, blocking my path to the door.

"Who is Simon, Melissa?" Her question stops me cold. How in the hell would she know about Simon.

"I don't know what you're talking about, Mandy. Is this a new man you plan on getting your hooks in?" Thank God, my voice comes out strong, despite how I feel on the inside. On the inside I am slowly dying. There is no way in hell she would know about Simon if it didn't come from Greg.

"Oh you stupid, stupid girl. Let me fill *you* in on what I know. Was your sister married? Hmm? Maybe married to Simon? Well, what you don't know and what your darling Greg is keeping from you, is that Simon was also married to *his* sister." It takes everything I have, every single ounce of control, not to react to her words. She doesn't wait before landing the final blow. "You know what he told me today? He told me he was sick of looking at you because every time he did all he could think about was how you are connected to the man who killed his sister. He couldn't stand to be around you any longer because you remind him of everything he hates." She spits the last word out and even though I'm sure all of the color has drained from my face, I stand my ground and offer her nothing.

"You will have to do better than that if you plan to scare me off, Mandy. Have a good night." I walk around her and down the hall. I don't even see the bar around me, or the patrons enjoying their meals and laughing at all the happiness in their world. The happiness in mine has just been stripped from my body. I feel completely gutted.

How does she know about Simon? She knows about Fia. And Grace? If I even could believe her, that means Greg has been keeping something huge from me. Grace was married to Simon? He knew this, the whole time I have been opening up to him about Cohen, my sister, her death... he knew who Simon was, and he knew who Cohen was.

Oh my God, he could have stopped him! As soon as the thought hits my brain, I almost fall over at the enormity of the situation. Greg's sister died over a decade ago and he knew Simon did it. He told me he disappeared after it happened, but if he would have stuck around and made sure Simon paid, then MY sister would still be here. My heart is pounding so quickly and my breathing is coming too fast. I have to get out of here.

I make it back to the table, but the girls must have had their eyes on me because they are up in a second and by my side.

"Meli? What's wrong?" Izzy, or maybe it was Dee, asks. I just shake my head and reach for my purse.

"Meli, please talk to us. What happened?" Pretty sure it was Dee that time.

"Is that fucking Mandy?" One of them asks and my body jolts at the name. I have to get out of here before Mandy sees that her words have had their desired effect. I can break down and lose it later, but I will be damned if I let her have the satisfaction of watching me do it.

"Not here," I croak and pull some cash from my wallet. After throwing it down, I take off to the door, making sure I don't give away to Mandy how upset I am.

I feel like someone has just removed my heart. My skin feels tight and my face hurts from holding my emotions in check. The burn that has taken up residence in my chest is making its way up my throat and I know that in seconds I won't be able to hold back the sobs.

"Meli, wait... please!" I can feel Izzy running up to me but I have my car in sight and escape on the horizon. "Melissa!"

She grabs my arm hard enough to prevent me from walking any further and turns me to her. I can feel my tears bubbling over, and when I open my mouth to tell her to drop it, I hardly recognize the sound that escapes. It's the sound of my heart shattering into millions of unbreakable pieces.

"Sweetie, what is going on?"

"Did you know?" I whisper, my voice wobbling and the tears still streaming down my face. "Did you know?" I ask again with more force.

She jerks back slightly at my question, her brow furrows, and she shakes her head, "Meli, I have no idea what you're talking about. Did I know what?"

I shake my head a few times and try to get to my car again. I don't know where Mandy is, but I know with that bomb, she isn't going to miss her chance to make sure it hit its mark. "I have to leave, Izzy. I can't be here when I fall apart." I beg.

"You can't drive either. Come on, you can come with me and I'll take you home."

"NO!" I start to force my way around her but she holds firm. Jesus... I have the size advantage on her short frame; how is she able to hold me back? "I'm not going home, not going to him!"

She seems even more confused at how fiercely I am refusing to go to Greg.

"Please, I can't go home." My strength is crumbling and my body is starting to shake with the effort it is taking to hold it in.

"Fine sweetie, that's fine. Come on. Let's figure out where you want to go while we're on the road, okay?"

She folds me in the seat, hands me my purse, and makes quick work in getting around the car and taking off. I have no idea where I am going to go, but I know I can't see Greg right now. At this point, I don't know if I will ever be able to face him again.

The last thing I see before we pull out of the lot is Mandy bursting through the front of Heavy's with Dee hot on her heels. She looks around but when she doesn't see what she is looking for, she turns on Dee and starts waving her hands around.

At least I'm out of there before she is able to watch me crumble. I can hear Izzy asking me where to go, and talk on her phone a few times, but I am in my own world. I pull my legs up toward my body and welcome the tears.

CHAPTER 22

Greg

When I wake up on the couch, I am slightly confused. The house is still dark and silent but glancing at the clock and seeing it is well past midnight, I know something is wrong. Melissa would never let me stay on the couch if she had already come home.

Damn, I am exhausted. I feel like the stress of keeping something from the girl I love is slowly eating at me. I know this talk isn't going to be easy, but it needs to be done. I just have to have enough faith in us and our love to know that she will be able to forgive me for keeping it from her.

Pulling myself off the couch and stretching my sore muscles from sleep, I take off in search for my girl. Maybe I didn't do such a good job letting her know that everything is okay. She knows something is off, but I don't think she could be so mad that she wouldn't come home. Sure, we have had our share of fights, but they have been over little things like leaving the lid off the toothpaste.

Ten minutes later, I am officially starting to worry. She isn't here. Not only is she not here, but it doesn't look like she's been here since before I got home. All of her stuff is still here, but she isn't.

I spend another ten minutes searching for my cell phone only to come up lacking. Jesus, I am losing my mind. I start to panic slightly when I realize if I don't have my phone, there is no way she would have been able to get a hold of me if something bad had happened. What if she was in an accident? Fuck! She could be in the hospital right now and I've been sleeping. I finally locate the little bastard under my seat in the truck, and almost fall to the ground when I see the amount of missed calls. One from Axel, one from Emmy, two from Dee, but it is the sixteen from Izzy that stops my heart.

When I finish going through all the messages, I still don't completely understand what is happening. Emmy seems confused and clueless. She lets me know that she didn't go out with the girls, but she did talk to Izzy and I need to call her as soon as possible. Dee's first message is just as confusing as Emmy's. Her second message, however, turns my blood to ice.

"G, I don't know what happened. Meli went to the bathroom and came out looking like she had just seen a ghost. She's gone but I do know Mandy did something. That little bitch isn't speaking though. You need to find her, G. Something's wrong but I don't know what. Call Izzy. She left with her a little while ago. Love you."

Mandy. What a motherfucking cunt. Who knows what she could have told Melissa but whatever it is, it couldn't be good. Why did I think she is done and over her obsession with my dick? The last chat I had with her had ended well enough. She apologized over and over and promised she wished me nothing but the best. I guess my first clue should have been when she mentioned getting back on her medication. Fuck.

When I listen to Izzy's messages that start out worried and end defeated, I know my bad luck has just turned to worse. She gives me nothing more than Dee did; apparently, my girl is locked up tight and not letting anyone in.

I am pacing the living room when Axel's message finally comes through the line.

"She's here and you need to stay away brother. I know this is going to be impossible for you, but trust me when I say she is safe, and I will make sure she stays that way. She knows, and when I say that, you know what I mean. Iz didn't say much, just that Mandy told her about Simon. Would love to know how that bitch knew enough to put your woman in this state. Let her cool and be here in the morning. And, G… if you tell Izzy I let you know she's here, I'll personally cut your dick off."

Thank Christ she is safe but that does nothing to ease the tension in my heart. I need to protect my girl; I need to be there. With not one care to the fact that it is way too late to be calling, I call Axel right back.

"What, motherfucker?" He grumbles in the phone.

"Is she okay?"

"What the fuck do you think? I have my woman in there with your woman because she hasn't stopped crying since she got here. I am not a chick and I like my dick so I didn't listen in for long but there was a lot of her saying shit I know she will regret and even more of her saying shit I know she won't."

"Not following, Axel. What are you saying?"

"What I'm saying is if you come over here right now, I don't think you will like what you get from her. She's hurt and I told you this would blow up, so I have to say I agree with her pain. But, she is also in shock. She's saying shit that I don't think she would be saying if she had a clear head. You love her, then you need to sit your fucking ass at home and let Izzy be the strength she needs."

"I don't know how to do that, Ax." I sigh and pull my hand through my hair. Every instinct I have is telling me to run, run to her, and pick up the pieces.

"I know you don't, but it's time to learn. You can't always be the one that makes it better. You can't protect everyone from everything. That's what got you in this mess." There is some shuffling in the background and I can hear him walking through his house, shutting some doors. "Let me look in on them. Will that help you a little?"

"Please," I whisper.

"Hold on." He sets the phone down, and after what seems like an eternity, I hear him pick back up and just sigh. "She's asleep. Curled up like a fucking baby in Izzy's arms. She's okay, G, but you have to give her this time. I'll call in the morning, yeah?"

"Ax, I don't know if I can do this. I feel like part of my soul is being ripped from my body."

"I know, trust me I do. I lived that for twelve years my man. The only thing I can give you is hope. Izzy and I went through our share of bumps, but in the end, if it's meant to be, nothing can keep your woman from your arms."

He disconnects and I sit there for hours, until the early rays of sunlight start filling the room. I sit there and think about what I'm going to do if I can't fix this, because right now I know I won't be able to recover if she doesn't want to be in my life anymore. It will be like losing Grace all over again.

I have been staring at one of the romance books Melissa left on the coffee table the night before, just zoning when the phone finally rings. Seeing that it is Axel, I have the phone connected and to my ear in seconds.

"Yeah?" Even to my own ears, I can hear the raw desperation that hangs from that single word.

"She left, Greg. I was changing Nate, and she and Izzy were downstairs. Gone for five minutes but when I got back down, she was already gone. Izzy won't tell me where she went because she said she just needs this time. Fuck, I'm sorry."

"She's gone?" I question.

"She's gone." With each word, the hope I have been hanging on to is slowly dying. "She didn't have her car here, so I think it would be a safe bet that one of the other girls has her. Didn't hear that from me though. I have to live with one of them and I would prefer to be whole. Check in, yeah?"

I don't know if I answered him. I might have, but when the dial tone's beep meets my ears, I wake up and disconnect the line. I sit there even longer wondering what the hell I'm supposed to do now.

I look back at the book sitting on the coffee table and wish that love was as easy as it is in romance books. Sure as shit would make what I am feeling right now a little bit easier if I know there is a happy ending right around the corner. Even the dude on the cover seemed to be mocking me. Looking at me like I should have known better than to even try to keep something from the woman I love. Fuck me, but I should have. I am getting ready to get up when I notice the title, *Withstanding Me* by Crystal Spears. Oh, irony… you really are a douchebag.

I make it about thirty minutes before I am in the truck and heading to Lilly's house. I'm not even expecting Melissa to be there but I need to speak with someone that's not attached to me as a friend. I need someone on her side that will understand her.

Since it is Tuesday and Cohen spends his mornings at a daycare center for some interaction with other children, I know it will be easier to have a chat with Lilly. I just hope like hell that she doesn't hate me when I finish laying it all out there.

"Greg? What are you doing here, honey?" Her smile is bright when she answers my knock, but as soon as she sees my face her smile drops and she wavers slightly before grabbing her chest. "Meli-Kate? Oh Lord, is my baby okay?"

"What? Oh God, Lilly... I'm sorry. I didn't even think what it would look like just showing up. She's okay. I just needed to talk."

"Oh, thank God. Sure thing, darling. Just come on in and let me get the laundry switched over."

I follow her down the short hallway and have a seat at the kitchen table. She brings in a load of towels and sits with a smile. "Alright, lay it out honey. Tell me what's on your mind."

"I don't even know where to start."

"In my experience, the best place is always the beginning," she says softly and pats my leg.

So, I do. I start from the beginning and tell her about Grace, how I dealt with Grace's death, starting the business, Izzy and her issues, and finally Melissa. Never once does she look at me with disgust. She sits there patiently listening to me lay it all out and just folds her towels. I expect her to kick me out when I tell her about how I knew Simon, but she just nods her head and continues folding. Finally, when I finish, I sit back and wait for it. Surely, she wouldn't want a piece of shit like me around her daughter.

"You have a good heart, Greg. I knew that the second you walked in the door with Cohen on your shoulders and a big smile on your face. Never once in the last month have I worried about Meli-Kate. Seems like all I've done since I lost my Sofia was worry about that girl. She wasn't happy and she didn't live. I saw her happiness come back when she met you. So I might not understand completely why you didn't just tell her in the beginning, but I know you didn't mean to hurt my baby."

"No ma'am, I would rather cut off my own arm than ever hurt her, but that's what I did anyway. Trying not to hurt her, I did and now I have no idea if it can be fixed."

"Sweet child, true love can always be fixed. When you love someone as much as you and my Meli-Kate love each other, there isn't a single mountain in the world too high to climb when things need to be fixed."

I take a deep breath and try to control the turbulence that is wreaking havoc on my body. "I can't lose her." And it is as simple as that. Losing her would be unimaginable.

"And you won't, dear. She needs time to process this. I know my girl, she is hurting, but she is staying away because she needs to figure out her head. Her heart will fix her quick and she'll be ready to talk."

For the first time since Axel's call this morning, I have a small feeling that maybe there is some hope and it will be okay. At this point, I have to believe that, because if Lilly isn't right, I don't know what I'll do.

"How do you not blame me, Lilly?" I whisper the words into my hand and almost hope that she misses them.

"Blame you for what exactly? Blame you for suffering a terrible loss? Oh, honey, you are just as big a victim here as we are. You lost someone you loved dearly, and no one would ever fault you for how you chose to deal with that. Everyone grieves differently. You did what you could to protect my Sofia even when you didn't know her, and honey, the only thing that does is make me love you a little more. None of this, what's happening with you and Meli-Kate, or what happened to your Grace or my Sofia should ever be on your shoulders to bear. Your heart has been in the right place all along; you just didn't realize it."

I haven't had a mother figure in my life for so long, and with everything that's happened since yesterday, it just becomes too much at that point. Knowing that Melissa's own mother doesn't look at me and wish me dead after knowing everything almost makes me feel like I have been forgiven for failing. I, for the first time since I lost Grace, don't feel the overwhelming sense of guilt.

"I'm sorry," I mumble before leaning forward and resting my face in my hands. "I'm sorry." It takes me a second to calm down, but she just sits there and softly brushes my hair while offering me reassuring words. There really is nothing in the world like a mother's touch, even when that mother isn't your own.

When I can finally control the whirlwind that is swirling around inside of me, I look up and meet her eyes.

She wipes her eyes with one of her towels and smiles sweetly at me. "Greg, if there was ever a doubt in my mind about how big that heart of yours is, you just proved it without question."

I stay with Lilly for a few hours and help her finish up some things around the house. I need to be around her, someone connected to Melissa, but I also need the comfort that she offers. When I leave she pulls me into a hug and wishes me luck.

The last place I want to go was home. I want to drive around Hope Town until I find my girl and carry her home. At this point, I feel like I could keep going until I meet ocean if it meant that I could get my girl in my arms. The need to have her in my arms is overwhelming, but I know Lilly was right. She needs time. So, I will be strong and give it to her.

I have only been home for a few minutes when I hear the front door click open. I instantly mute the TV, and stand from the couch, waiting to see who is coming down the hall. It could be one of the boys but I am praying it will be Melissa.

When she walks into sight, my knees get weak and I almost have to sit down. Even though I can see she is upset, she is still the most beautiful thing I have ever laid eyes on.

"Hey," she offers weakly.

"Beauty," I whisper, "God, baby."

CHAPTER 23
Melissa

When I walk in the door, I half expect him to charge me, but when I find him standing in the middle of the living room looking worse than I feel, I can't help but feel like a world class bitch for disappearing on him. But I needed the time. Time to sort my head and time to make sure that I don't do or say something I can't take back. If I would have seen him before, then there really is no telling where we would be right now. I just know it wouldn't be pretty.

He looks like he has been through the wringer. and didn't come out the victor. He is standing there in the same clothes he wore to work the day before; his hair is all over the place as if he has ran his hands through it over and over. But it isn't his clothes or hair that make me pause; it's his eyes. Those bright baby blues that I have fallen in love with look shattered. His handsome face is pale with a full day's growth of beard, and his bloodshot eyes have dark circles underneath. My night might have been hard, but something tells me that his has been even worse.

We just stand there for a few minutes, feeling unsure of where we both stand, but when I see a single tear fall down his cheek, I am done with the distance. Dropping my keys and purse to the floor, I take off and rush into his arms.

"I'm sorry, so sorry," he whispers brokenly into my hair.

"I know." I do, after letting it all out last night and feeling as though my world had ended. When I woke up this morning, and the pain had faded but the anger hadn't. I know in my heart that Greg would never intentionally hurt me but it still stings. Out of all the garbage that Mandy had thrown at my feet last night, I know he wouldn't have said all of that to her. He might have mentioned Simon, in whatever capacity, but he never would have spoken about me... about us, like that. It is easier to begin to understand his motivation when I put that past me.

After I had Emmy pick me up this morning and take me back to Heavy's to get my car, I drove straight to Fia's grave and talked to the one person who I knew would get me.

Hours. I spent hours laying on the cool grass next to my sister's grave and talked to her. It wasn't easy talking to someone who wasn't able to talk back to you, but I needed her and this was the best place.

When I finished my chat with Fia's cold tombstone, I had realized one thing. This man would do anything to protect me. He would protect my body with his own. And he would protect my feelings and my heart by keeping something from me that could be damaging. I knew that he was doing what he felt was the right thing. Didn't make it right, but it is what it is.

In the end, I had to ask myself if I could live without this man in my life just because he kept something from me. And no, there is no way I could give him and what we have just because of this.

"I didn't think you would come back," he mumbles against my neck. He gives me a soft kiss and inhales loudly. "I would have hunted you down by dinner; giving you space was the hardest thing I have done in a long time."

"I know. I needed to clear my head."

"I'm so sorry. You have no idea how sorry I am that I didn't just tell you, but we were new and I didn't know how you would handle it, baby. I had planned on telling you; I just didn't know how." His eyes are searching mine, begging me to hear his words. "I hurt you and it is eating me alive."

"Stop, please?" His lips clamp shut and I bring my hand up to run my fingers across them softly. His eyes continue pleading with me, asking for forgiveness that he doesn't need. "I understand now, why you did it and it's okay. Last night I was so far in my own head that it would have been terrible if I had come right home. I am so sorry for running but I *had* to. I know it sounds childish but I had to."

"I was afraid you would blame me. Fuck, I've been doing it to myself for years, so why wouldn't you?" I'm clearly confused now because I can't figure out for the life of me why I would blame him for not telling me that he knew Simon. Sure, the thought filtered through my mind in anger last night that he could have somehow prevented Fia's death, but even I know how ludicrous that is in the light of day.

"Baby, what could I possible blame you for? Having a hard time dealing with the loss of your sister? I did too; hell, I still do. Not telling me about our connection through that son of a bitch? I don't blame you for that. I understand you thought it was the best and, baby…I can't say for sure, but if you would have sprung that on me right away, I might have freaked out."

"Doesn't make it right, Beauty. I hurt you." His words hit my heart and the love I feel for this man just grows. He has torn himself to pieces because he indirectly hurt me. Whatever I did to deserve a man like him, I feel blessed that I am even allowed a gift like that. I place my hands on both sides of his scruffy face and pull him down to my lips. It's just a soft meeting of our mouths, but enough for him to feel my love and assurance that we are okay.

"My feelings were hurt, but Greg, you can't protect me from everything. Even you will hurt my feelings every now and then. What's important is that you don't keep things from me. We are a team, and from now on, it's complete honesty, okay?"

"Love you so much, baby." He says softly before kissing me deeply.

He continues to devour my lips in a kiss that is almost bruising. He is letting out everything he has felt over the last twenty-four hours and pouring it into this kiss. I feel owned, loved, cherished, and branded. His hands are frantic against my body, pulling my shirt over my head and in his haste to get my bra unhooked, he snaps the clasp clear off the bra. He pauses long enough to pull his shirt over his head, and that gives me enough time to shed my jeans and underwear. Before I can even blink, he has me backed up to the wall and his lips back on mine. His hands roam over my skin, causing it to get tight, and a chill to flash through my body. I love the feel of his hard body against my softness. How his hard muscles feel against my fingertips.

My lips feel bruised and swollen by the time he pulls back and locks eyes with me. He looks nothing like the man that I saw when I walked in the door. This man standing before me now is my beast.

"I need to show you my love, Beauty."

After that line, I am confused when he drops to his knees, but when I feel his hands dig into my hips and lift, I do the only thing I can. Push my back against the wall and wrap my legs over his shoulders. He wastes no time gripping my ass tight and locking his mouth to my pussy. Two seconds later, I am fisting his hair tight and pushing him closer while my release rushes through me. He continues sucking and licking, pulling me closer to his mouth.

"Baby, can't—I can't," I whimper.

"You will," he says against my dripping pussy. "You can."

He lifts me higher and dips his tongue deep, dragging it back slowly toward my clit, and circling the swollen bud before taking it between his lips and sucking. He repeats the process twice before I am screaming my second release. I can feel my wetness against his face when he turns his head and kisses each of my thighs before helping me stand. More like helping me lean against the wall so he can stand up.

"When did you take off your pants?" I question when he stands to his full height and his dick stands tall and proud between us. The piercings in the tip stand out against his tan stomach, bumping against his belly button. I lick my lips and he growls.

"Between the first and second time you came all over my tongue. Did you not feel me let go of your ass?"

"Um, baby... I was a little busy."

"Yeah, and it was delicious." He gets close again and picks me up, and I wrap my legs around his hips. His thick erection immediately seeks entrance. "Watch me love you." He pulls his hips back slightly, and I reach between our bodies and help guild him inside me. He settles deep and quick with one thrust, and my head falls back with a thud against the wall.

With his hands on my hips and mine against his shoulders, our lips connect and our bodies lock together. We move as if we have been doing this mating dance for years. It doesn't take long before he pulls back to look into my eyes, and the love I see reflected is enough to push me over the edge. He pushes me back down and rolls his hips a few times before I feel his warm release against the walls of my pussy.

"You're such a beast," I speak softly into his ear before nipping his lope lightly with my teeth.

"But I'm your beast, and baby… every Beauty needs a Beast."

"Yeah, I sure do." I laugh and wrap my arms around his neck. "I love you."

"I love you too. So much, baby." His warm breath hits my neck and with our bodies still locked together, I know that we will be okay. Our love might be new, but it is powerful enough overcome.

CHAPTER 24
Melissa

(3 Months Later)

Waking up wrapped tight within Greg's arms is the best feeling in the world. Even in sleep, he keeps his arms tight around my torso and his legs tangled with mine. My beast. Always ready for anything.

I lift his arm, detangle my legs from his, and slowly slide out of the bed. When I turn to look at him, expecting to find him asleep, his eyes are open and staring at me with a hint of humor dancing in their depths.

"Where are you going, Beauty?" His voice is thick with sleep and just the sound of it shoots straight through my body.

Slipping one of his shirts over my head, I turn around and try to keep a stern face, but fail after only a few seconds. "You could at least make it a little easier to sneak out and make you breakfast."

"Babe, seriously? You're already in bed, so that kind of defeats the purpose of giving me my breakfast when you *leave* the bed."

Such. A. Man.

"I hate to point out the obvious, but three year olds don't sleep in. Since we're pushing 8:00, I think we are lucky he hasn't come running in yet." Greg groans and rolls over at the reminder that Cohen is just down the hall. "I think I hear little feet, baby. You might want to get up and put some pants on. I'm thinking if Cohen gets one look at the size of your dick, we are going to have questions for days, not to mention those delicious decorations you're rocking there."

He gets up laughing, but before grabbing his briefs and covering himself up, he folds me in his arms and gives me one hell of a good morning kiss. We are just pulling apart when the door swiftly opens, banging against the wall, and Cohen comes flying in. Cape and all.

"Melwee? What are you doing? Why is Greg not wearing his big boy underwear? Why doesn't Greg have clothes on? I wanna be naked! You're gonna see his wiener, and Nana said that boys shouldn't show their wieners to girls. It's naughty. You're gonna go to time out." Sometimes I wonder if breathing is even a requirement for a three year old. I mean, does he want me to answer that? I don't think so.

I can feel Greg laughing against my back, trying to hide himself behind my body so that we don't have even more of Cohen's one hundred questions. "A little help here?" He whispers in my ear.

"Cohen, did you hear that? I think there is a ninja downstairs! Let's go check it out." And like magic, he's off. Doesn't take much. One mention of bad guys to fight, and he is instantly ready to protect the world. It amazes me daily how much Cohen is turning into a mini-Greg. With years of no manly figures in his life, I feel beyond blessed to be able to give this to him.

Over the last three months, the bond between Greg and Cohen has become something that even I don't have a factor in. He spends more time here than he does with my mom. There are weeks that I have to drag them apart because Greg can't let go. Forget the actual child; I have to deal with a thirty-five year old man pitching a fit because his little buddy is going back to Nana's house.

"Meet you downstairs, baby." I give him a quick kiss before taking off to find my little warrior.

Ever since the incident with Mandy, Greg and I have become even closer. It seems odd that we have formed this type of relationship so quickly but when we are together, no one else in the world matter. He once told me I was his missing piece to the puzzle, and he wasn't wrong. How I ever thought I would be able to withstand the charms of this man is beyond me.

Mandy isn't an issue anymore, thank God. Greg has tracked down her father. He is high enough up the political ladder that the last thing he needs is his daughter causing trouble. Greg called and explained the situation. According to daddy dearest, the reason that she has been silent for so long is because he has admitted her to some intensive program that deals with severe bipolar disorder. I personally think that they might want to re-evaluate her for some more shit. There is no way I am buying his excuse. She was two steps away from turning serial killer and trapping Greg in a hole, making him 'put the lotion on' every few hours, like that guy in the movie *Joe Dirt*.

I don't care either way what happens to her as long as she leaves us the hell alone. Sure, it would be nice to see her ass in jail becoming someone's bitch, but I want it done. I want her gone so that I can enjoy my happy ever after.

The guard will always be up when it comes to her, but for the most part, we are just ready to move on.

A week after we had made up with the best wall sex turned marathon loving, I had officially broken the lease at my apartment and moved in. The way I see it is life is too short to sit on your ass and not live every minute as if it's your last. Greg is my future and I'm not going to wait to start living it.

We spend a lot of time talking about our sisters, and how we feel they had a hand in bringing us together. Whether it was them, fate, or just damn good luck, we both agree that we are beyond lucky.

Mom has agreed that with things going so well between Greg and myself, it is time to finally get started on fulfilling Fia's wish that I have custody of Cohen. It isn't any issue to start the ball rolling, but there are still hoops we need to jump through and red tape to cut. Regardless of the time it will take, soon enough my little guy will be calling this house home. It is hard to tell who is more excited, me or them.

We had our first meeting with child protective services last week and Greg is positive that things went well. We can provide Cohen a stable and comfortable life. We are both young, and have no blemishes on our background. It helps that we learned that the lady that came out to do our first home study has a son in the Marines. When Greg mentioned that he was honored to meet the mother of such a brave man, I thought I would lose it. They started discussing various concerns that she had about her baby being overseas, and that, in turn, ended up being one of those conversations that ended up so emotional that I had to excuse myself. When she left, Greg gave me the reassurance I needed, but excused himself for a few hours.

We talk about his time spent serving, but usually, he is very short with his answers. He told me once that it isn't that he doesn't want to tell me, but that he just can't. He is a proud man and never shies away from telling me what it was like for him to be serving his country, but he doesn't like to talk about it. The details are never deep; we just touch on how he felt during those eight years. It is one of those things that he will talk about when I ask him, but I can see the pain that is there, so I don't question him often.

I walk past Cohen's new bedroom at the end of the hall and continue downstairs with a smile on my face. I still couldn't believe how much my life has changed in just a few short months.

How's this for living, Fia?

"Melwee! I got them, got them all! Can I have Coco Puffs this morning?"

"Good for you, C-Man!" I give him a high five and continue to the fridge. "No Coco Puffs, baby. We're

223

making Greg's favorite today." I turn around expecting a smile, because at the mention of chocolate chip pancakes, that's usually the reaction that follows. But he is sitting at the table just looking at me. No emotion shows, but his little brows crease, and his lips push out in the adorable little pout he always makes when he's thinking.

"What's going on in that super brain of yours?" I ask, starting the prep for breakfast. He's silent for so long that I stop what I'm doing and look up. He is still in the same position. "Cohen, baby, what's wrong?" I put everything down and turn off the burner, making my way around the island and crouching on the floor in front of him.

"Melwee, why don't I have a daddy?" The normal happy and carefree tone that is always present has been replaced with a sort of sadness I don't think I've ever heard in my nephew's voice.

"Oh, Cohen, you had a daddy baby, and he loved you very much." I almost have to choke on the words to get them out. "But your daddy is an angel now, remember? He and your mommy are angels and God told them that they are the luckiest angels in all of heaven because they get to sit on the brightest cloud and watch over you."

"But how come my daddy can't come and play with me like Greg does?" he asks with all the innocence of a child.

I stand up and pull him into my arms before sitting back down in his seat. "Cohen baby, sometimes God wants people to learn to fly even when we aren't ready. He wanted your daddy to get his wings and fly so that he could be an angel in heaven. When people get their wings and go to heaven, they can't come back and play with us. I know it isn't fair baby, but that doesn't mean that your daddy doesn't still love you."

"And mommy. Don't forget mommy. She loves me too, you said so. She loves me to the moon and the stars and everything in between."

"She sure does, little man." I give him a hug, and with his small arms wrapped around my neck, I reach up and brush the tear off my cheek. Right when I get ready to pull back, I look up and meet Greg's eyes from where he is standing in the doorway, watching us with a small smile. I start to give him one back when Cohen's next question stops me.

"So does that mean that Greg is gonna be my daddy?" Greg eyes widen slightly and his mouth parts with a small 'O'. I, on the other hand, have been stunned silent. "Melwee, can Greg be my daddy and you be my mommy now? I really wanna have a daddy, but only if you can be my mommy."

"Oh, baby," I whisper and pull him close again. I don't realize how tight I have been hugging him until he laughs and wiggles out of my lap.

"You're face looks funny, Melwee." He laughs, and when he turns around and sees Greg standing there, his whole little body lights up and he takes off running. "GREG! Did you hear? You're gonna be my daddy because I want to have the best daddy in the world."

"Yeah, C-Man, I heard. I think that's best present anyone has ever given me." He leans forward and kisses him on the head before ruffling his hair. "Run to the bathroom and wash your hands real fast. Make sure you get off all those yucky ninja germs."

"Okay… Daddy," he whispers the last word and takes off to the half bath off the garage entrance.

My eyes haven't left Greg's once, and when I see his eyes start to get heavy with unshed moisture, I lose it. I'm sure I look a mess, and Cohen would take great pleasure in reminding me how funny my face looks now.

"Beauty, get over here." His soft rumble fills my ears and I rush into his arms.

"Are you okay?" I ask when I calm down.

"Better than okay. Greatest moment in my life, next to meeting you, was hearing that little boy call me his dad. I love him just as much as I love you, Melissa, and that moment was one to celebrate. Stop the tears. Okay, baby?"

"You're happy?" When I look up and see his eyes clear and his smile blinding, I know that right here in our kitchen, with the smell of chocolate chip pancakes in the air, we just became a family.

"Happiest man in the world."

"I love you." I whisper.

"Love you back, Beauty. Now get over there and make your men some food."

I turn on a laugh and jump slightly when he smacks my ass, but when we hear Cohen's laugh, we both look over at him. "Told you that you were gonna go to time out! You shouldn't look at wieners, Melwee!"

We spend the day at the Georgia Aquarium and have some time with just the three of us. This is pretty normal for a Sunday when we know Cohen is going to go stay at my mom's for the week. Greg has a lot of stuff going on at the office and won't be able to take Cohen in with him for a few days. Now that we have started having Cohen over more and more, it is getting harder to drop him off with my mom. I know she sees it too, but we are managing.

Tonight we are headed out for 'family' dinner with the Corps Crew at Heavy's. This is also something that we have all started to do at least once a month. It seems as though these men get broody when they go too long without their bonding over beer time. It works out perfect for the girls in the group. Let's face it, there really is only so much time you can spend on the phone with the same girls on group calls yelling over each other.

We are the last ones to arrive and squeeze into the table. Our seats end up directly across from Izzy, Axel and Nate. Next to Izzy is Dee and on the other side of Axel is Coop. I have pushed up to Maddox when I sit down and get a lift of his chin in greeting. Emmy is on the other side of Coop, next to Greg. Cohen leaves our side right away to sit next to Nate. Even though Nate is only a freshly turned one year old, he is Cohen's best bud. When Cohen is around, Nate's face never leaves his.

"Izzy, what do you want to bet those two are already taking notes on future ways to give us gray hair?" I laugh when their heads go close and Cohen starts babbling at a smiling Nate.

"That I don't doubt, girlfriend. You look happy today." She nods her head at Greg and gives me a wink.

"Oh yeah, I'll fill you in tomorrow, okay?" She smiles and looks over my shoulder across the room.

I turn to see what holds her attention and watch in shock as Beck leans over to give an attractive woman at the bar a kiss. Well, that explains the look on Dee's face.

Turning back around, I catch Izzy's gaze with wide eyes. I have heard from her and Emmy that his way of pushing Dee into admitting she does, in fact have feelings for him is to make her jealous. Izzy gives me a small shake of her head and immediately changes the subject to everyone's plans for Halloween.

I look over at Dee while the rest of the table talks about having some kind of party; no thank you... I hate Halloween. Her eyes haven't left Beck, even when he returns to the table and squeezes in between Greg and Emmy. She just continues to give him her death rays. After a few minutes, she takes a deep breath and joins the conversation around her.

Crisis averted apparently.

"Daddy!" It takes me a second to realize that that was coming from our table. When I realize that everyone has stopped talking around us, and Greg had curled his hand that is resting on my leg tight, that yes, that voice has indeed come from our table.

"Yeah, buddy?" He asks Cohen.

I take a second to look up at the faces around the table. Dee looks confused, which is understandable since I'm sure her mind is still processing Beck's latest attempt at calling her bluff. Izzy already has tears rolling down her cheeks. Axel, Emmy, and Coop all have the same shocked but happy face. Beck is still glaring at Dee, so it's a safe bet him missed it. I finish my rotation and look to my side at Maddox. For the first time since I've met him, his face has a blinding smile, the kind of smile that completely transforms his face from unapproachable to sinfully handsome.

Wow.

"When I get big like you, will my wiener be big too?" Jesus Christ. Really, way to end a moment there kid.

Greg, even though he did tries, can't hold in the laughter at Cohen's question. Soon the whole table is laughing. I see Maddox lean over, motion Cohen forward, and then I watch as he whispers something in his ears. Cohen smiles and shakes his head rapidly a few times. His little hand shoots up and meets Maddox's large paw in a five before he returns to his 'conversation' with Nate.

"What did you say?" I ask Maddox softly when he leans back into his seat.

He turns his black eyes on me, with that blinding smile still present. "Told him to eat all his greens, and be a good little boy, and he would have the biggest wiener in town."

I sit there with my jaw on the ground, completely shocked that I just got not only a smile, but also a joke from this man, before I throw my head back and laugh. Greg wraps his arm around my shoulders and pulls me close. It takes me a while to stop laughing and be able to sit back and enjoy our family dinner.

We didn't stay long, but when we go to leave, I get a long hug from Izzy with demands for a phone call first thing in the morning. Axel and Greg did that man hug for a few minutes, and I can see Axel's head turned speaking into Greg's ear. When they break apart I see Greg's hand go up and wipe his eyes. I'll let him have his moment. I know how much this day has meant to him, so having Cohen call him out in the middle of the people closest to him has to be hitting him emotionally.

We make it to mom's house with enough time to give Cohen his bath for her and tuck him into bed. While Greg is reading him a story, I fill my mom in on the day we had. She has tears in her eyes when Greg returns but doesn't say anything. We make plans for dinner in a few days, and leave shortly after Cohen falls asleep. When she gives me a hug goodbye, she whispers in my ear how happy she is that Cohen is finally getting a daddy worth having.

The ride home is silent but comfortable. And when we get home, the silence continues until Greg has me naked, straddling his hips, and screaming out his name.

The perfect end to a perfect day.

CHAPTER 25
Melissa

When the phone wakes me up from a deep sleep, I jump in bed and almost fall off the side. Greg is already reaching over and tagging the phone off the side table by the time I have righted myself on the bed and calmed my heart a little.

Jesus, who the hell calls at four in the morning?

"Cage," I hear him rumble. In a moment of silence, his voice has lost all the rough sleepy sound, and he barks his next words with so much venom, my eyes snap to him in shock. "What. Did. You. Say?"

When he tosses the covers back, throws a shirt in my direction, and starts pulling on his own clothes, I know that this isn't going to be just a pleasant wake up call. Something is wrong. He would never pull me out of bed like this.

"When?" He barks into the phone, frozen as if turned to stone with his pants only up to his knees, and looks over at me. When I see fear in his eyes, I know that this is not going to be good. "Get fucking over there now, Coop. Call local on the way and figure out what you can. Now, Coop." He pulls the phone away, and after dropping it down on the floor, walks over to me. "Baby, it's going to be okay, yeah?"

"You're scaring me, Greg." I just look at him and wait for him to spit it out. "Who is it?"

"Coop got a call from the monitoring company in charge of your mom's security system. You remember the system I put in a few months ago? Wired it straight to our servers so all distress calls get reported to us as well as the local authorities. Shit, baby. Someone pressed the panic button. Coop called me first, but he doesn't know anything else. Get dressed and let's make sure everything is okay."

When I clearly can't force the moves on my own, he helps me pull on my clothes and guides me out to the truck. We make the trip across town to into the neighborhood where my mom lives in less than ten minutes. When we turn on her street and see her house lit up with all the emergency vehicles surrounding, it my heart stops and I know I'm going to be sick.

"Stop the truck! STOP IT NOW," I scream and slam my hand over my mouth. He pulls over and stops the car. By the time he makes it around to my side, I have already lost the contents of my stomach all over the sidewalk.

"Baby, stay here and let me go see what's going on okay?" I know he is trying to do what's best, but no, that is my family in that house.

"NO! We do this together. I need to know, Greg. I need to know what is happening and I can't be without you when I find out."

"Right. Come on, baby, and stay at my side."

We walk the few feet left between where he pulled over and the police tape begins. I have to fight every instinct in me to keep from running straight for the front door to find my mom and Cohen and make sure they are okay. He looks around for a few seconds until I hear him calling someone over. I don't hear the words; my eyes focus only on the open front door, watching as a dozen or so uniformed men walk in and out of my mother's house.

I don't even realize that I am shivering until Greg pulls me to his side and wraps me in his arms. I can feel his voice against my ear, but I still can't make out the words. After a few seconds, I feel his body tense and look up into his eyes.

Even in the dark of the night and the odd shadows the flashing lights make on his face, I can tell he has lost all the color in his skin. He looks pale, hollow, and pained.

"What? What is it?"

"We need to get to the hospital, baby." He looks down at me and I can see it there in his face that he isn't telling me everything.

"Tell me now, Greg. I can't take the not knowing." The tears are already coming quick and I can feel the sobs starting to bubble up. "Tell me now, dammit!" I scream.

"Your mom, baby, she's been hurt, and we need to get over there." He's still not telling me everything. His own tears are starting to fill his eyes, and he blinks a few times, trying to compose himself the best he can. "It's Cohen baby, he's—he's not here."

I don't hear anything else after that. I feel my body hit wave after wave of bone chilling cold. I hear Greg calling out my name, and feel him reach out to grab me as my vision dims and my body crumbles.

Greg

For what feels like the millionth time, I look over at Melissa, her body curled tightly around her legs, much like the last nine hours. She looks so small sitting here in the stark hospital waiting room. With both her legs pulled up tight against her body, and her arms constricting them in place, she hugs herself, her eyes staring off into the distance, but not seeing anything. I'm not even sure if she is emotionally still here in the room.

Maddox and Coop just left with news I did not want to hear. It looks as if Simon Wagner has reach, even from the grave. The monitoring system that I had installed at Lilly's house is the best of the best. We had learned a valuable lesson after what we'd gone through with Izzy's ex-husband a few years ago. Now, there's a camera on every entry point to her house. When it comes to my family, I won't take any chances.

Maddox pulled the security footage, and when he found out what happened to Cohen, I was the first person he called. It seems that Susan Wagner hasn't gone away quietly as we had originally thought. He explained that in the film she is walking up with an unidentified man, and after a few minutes of working on the door, makes her way inside. Things are quiet for about five minutes before he sees her running back out with Cohen in her arms. He doesn't have to say it but I can tell by his tone that it hadn't been pretty. I only know that Cohen was awake, alert, and appeared to be unharmed.

That little reassurance is all I have to go on right now.

The man that had entered the house with Susan Wagner had spent another ten minutes or so inside before coming back out. Best guess was that Susan had hired him to take care of Lilly while she snatched Cohen. Coop is monitoring the police scanners but so far, there haven't been any sightings of them. There is an Amber Alert going out as we speak but we all fear it's too late to stop her from crossing state lines.

Before they left, they let me know that, after looking into Susan's background, their best guess is that she is heading west to the Vegas area, the last known location of her sister, Ann.

Lilly has been in surgery for the last eight hours and it isn't looking good. When Izzy arrived a few hours ago, I set off to get some information on Lilly. I had hoped to offer Melissa some hope, but that thought quickly vanished when I learned how grave the situation was.

She suffered not only a blow to the head, but also multiple stab wounds and several vital organs had been affected. It wasn't looking good, but I couldn't give up hope, and I damn sure couldn't show how much I was dying inside when I needed to be strong for my girl.

The only thing I can do now is make sure I got our boy home.

I walk back over to Melissa and kneel in front of her. Her eyes meet mine but she doesn't focus until I call her name a few times.

"Beauty, I'm going to make a call right now. Izzy's going to stay right here with you okay?"

She just looks into my eyes; all the light that is normally shining back at me is gone. Her eyes are flat and her expression locked tight in grief.

"Okay, baby. I'll be right back." I lean forward and kiss her forehead, holding my lips there for a few moments before standing. I squeeze Izzy's shoulder and walk out into the hallway.

There is only one man that can possibly help me now. If Susan Wagner has taken Cohen, threatened my family, and possibly taken my woman's mother from her life, I will stop at nothing to make sure that I not only get Cohen back, but that Susan fucking Wagner won't ever be a threat to my family again.

It takes me a few seconds to control myself enough to dial a number I haven't used in years.

"Breaker." I hear snap through the line.

"It's Cage. Break... Neck. Fucking breakneck." I wait, choking down the ball of worry that threatens to escape. After I lost Grace and took off, I hooked up with

Braxxon Breaker out west. His MC club had been on a charity ride and we just happened to cross paths at the right time. After a night of partying, I decided to stick with them for a few days and enjoy the benefits that come with a bunch of bikers. To this day, I know I have a brother for life in Braxxon Breaker, and just because it's been years, that doesn't mean he won't come running with one word.

"Cage, brother. What's up?" He doesn't sound pissed that I cut into his time now. Curious maybe, but not angry.

"Cuts me fucking deep needing to make this call, Braxx. Got a situation and it isn't a situation I can take care of." There isn't anything else that needs to be said. He knows what I'm saying without actually saying it.

"Name it, brother." He says. I hear some shuffling in the background so I wait a second to respond.

"My girl, fuck… there isn't enough time to explain the six degrees of fucked up I've found myself in. My girl's nephew. The other grandparent took him, snatched him right out of bed, and did not leave anything pretty behind. Her mother is critical and questionable. Best I can find is she took him your way. Braxx, I won't let anyone hurt what is mine. Never again. This ends." By the time I get it all out, my control is slipping even more. I manage to sound a whole hell of a lot calmer than I actually am. I can't lose it, not here, and not before I have Cohen locked tight in my arms.

"Cage, brother, I need you to say what you need from me?"

"I'll be in Vegas in twelve hours, tops. Got to find my boy and bring him home. I wouldn't be making this call if I didn't need you. Turn that shit red, Braxx." There will be no doubt left when this is done. Susan Wagner will not fuck with what's mine and walk away clean.

It only takes a second before his deep rumble hits my ear. "It's done, Breakneck. Headed that way. Dial me again when in Vegas."

"As soon as I land. Owe you big, brother." There will never be a way to repay this debt, but I will gladly hand over anything he wants in payment if it means my family is in my arms, whole and safe.

When I hear the line go dead, I make my way back inside and pull Melissa into my arms. We continue to sit there, staring at the door, and waiting for news on Lilly.

CHAPTER 26
Greg

It is almost impossible to pull myself away from Melissa. About an hour after I called Braxxon, we get the news that her mother didn't make it. Holding her in my arms while she screams with pain and grief is heartbreaking. Knowing all too well how it feels like to lose your parent, the only one you have left, I know how her heart is suffering. I hold her tight and keep reminding her how much I love her and that I will find Cohen. With every tear and wail that comes from her body, my heart splits a little more.

When it finally becomes apparent that she isn't going to be able to calm down on her own, we have the doctor admit and sedate her. She is resting peacefully when I bend over and press my lips to her lax ones.

I don't want to leave her when I know she would need me the most, but what matters now is finding Cohen and getting him back safely in her arms. Neither of us would survive the hit that losing him would give us. With Izzy's assurance to keep me updated, I make my way home to pack a bag and get to the airport.

By the time I land in Vegas, I have been awake for over twenty-four hours. No sleep is needed when you are running on pure fucking adrenaline and hope.

I walk out the doors into the desert sun and lock eyes with the man I've come to see.

Braxxon Breaker. In the flesh.

"Braxx," I say, not even slightly ashamed when my voice catches. He looks the same as he did when we were both in our younger twenties and running through booze and women like there was no tomorrow. And those days, for me, there wasn't. Fuck, it would be nice to see him without this cloud of shit. "Thanks for coming, brother."

"Cage, don't give me that shit. You call Breakneck, my ass be here in a heartbeat. Brothers, man, brothers."

"Regardless, you're here when you don't have to be. You know what I'm asking and you still came... so that deserves my thanks." Stubborn son of a bitch, now I remember what it was that connect us. "You remember Locke? Did what he does best, and got a general area that bitch took my boy. Not going to be easy, from what I can tell they're hiding out right off the strip." I watch his eyes to see if the information even fazes him. Not sure why I think it will, but I need to make sure he is down with what I need.

He shoves off the white van he's leaning against and walks the few feet that separate us. He offers me a small smile, the rings in his lip flashing in the sunlight. "That general location, you know how many may be in there? I need numbers, brother. I work best with numbers." His voice is flat, but laced with the heat I need, and the power that he will stand behind his promise. You call Breakneck and it is top priority. He needs his intel, but that doesn't stop the confidence from coming through his tone loud and clear.

"Van," I say and nod my head toward his ride. "Nice, Braxx, all we need is the bag of candy now." He might have muttered asshole under his breath, but he walks around the back and slides into the seat.

"Van's hot, no trace," he offers when he settles in and waits for me to continue.

"Alright, Susan Wagner, age unknown and not important. Cohen Wagner, age three and my boy and target. Ann Matthews, sister to Susan and the only connection we have between Susan and Vegas. Male of unknown age is also with them. That bastard cut my woman's mom up Braxx; that motherfucker suffers. I don't think there is anyone else helping. This bitch is not stupid, but she isn't smart either."

"Alright, brother. Your kid, he might not take kindly to me. I hate to say this, shit I hate to say this, but you need to ride with. You feel me?" Like he even has to mention it. The only thing that is keeping me going right now is the thought that Cohen will be in my arms soon.

We head off towards an area near Naked City; from what Coop has told me, this area is high in crime, drugs, and prostitution, your typical urban setting, with small apartments, clustered shit-holes, and some 7-Elevens sprinkled in between. Kids that should be in school are selling drugs on the street, and bitches that look like they are on their death beds are begging for you to pull over. This is not an area you want to be in.

"Jesus Fucking Christ," I mutter into the window. I don't want to be here but I damn sure don't want Cohen here. "We have to find him, Braxx."

"Cage, you know me, man. I don't fuck around. We're gonna getcha boy back." His voice is no longer questioning. His tone is not only dripping in confidence and fury, but I can feel the compassion coming off him in waves. Braxxon might be the one man I know not afraid to get his hands dirty, but his heart is pure fucking gold when it comes to someone he considers his family.

Braxx doesn't offer anything else, but then again, neither do I. We crawl through the streets that make up Naked City and wait. Wait for the call in, but look for any sign that might lead us to my boy.

We have been driving around aimlessly for the last thirty or so minutes when the call finally comes in. 'C.S. Control' flashes across the screen, letting me know that one of the boys had found something.

"Cage," I bark in the phone. My patience is slowly wearing off with each passing homeless person, prostitute, or thug we pass. I can't stand the thought of Cohen's innocence being fucked with by these people. The thought of my boy alone and scared is eating me alive. "Speak, Goddammit."

"It's Coop. Maddox found him. Well, Maddox found where he should be. Sister's dead husband has some property just north of where you are now. I've got you pulled up on the GPS so just keep taking that road North and I'll let you know when to turn."

"Got it," I respond to Coop. "Keep north until I get word," I rattle off to Braxx. No fucking way I'm bringing his name up to Coop. Maddox is the only one who knows who I met up with, and that's one person too many.

"Greg, who the fuck are you with?" Coop questions.

"None of your business. Just keep your eyes on the screen and tell me how to get to my boy." Yeah. Patience is gone.

"Jesus Christ, you're going to get locked up or worse, Greg. I hope you know what you're doing."

"I've got it taken care of. Are we close?" Shut this shit down; I have to shut it down. I take a few deep breaths and wait for the signal to turn. After a few more minutes, we find ourselves sitting in front of the nastiest piece of shit I have ever seen in my life. How this house is still standing is beyond me. Boxes of shit line the front, and more trash and used junk cars litter the yard, but what I don't see is people. Not one single vehicle that looks like it's running is in the yard. Just shit, Christmas lights and cats.

"Cage, stay put man. I know that'll eat at ya, knowing your boy is in there. But this is why I'm here. I'll be back. In the meantime, grab my black saddlebag outta the back of the van. Unzip it for me, will ya? Grab a gun, just in case. It's unmarked, no ties, if you should happen to need it. Leave the bag unzipped. My favorite toys are in there. And somethin' tells me I'm about to play." He lets out a few low laughs that are pure evil, and not for the first time, I find myself glad to call him a friend and not an enemy. Braxxon Breaker is not an enemy you want to have.

"Greg? What the fuck are you doing?" I hear Coop call over the line. *Fuck.*

"Forget you heard that, Zeke Cooper, and don't you fucking tell me you wouldn't do everything possible to make sure you came out the victor in this situation. Not going to let my woman or our family be threatened again." He starts to speak but I disconnect and throw my phone down on the seat, waiting to climb out quietly and make my way to the back to follow Braxx's directions. Folding myself back in the seat, I watch him move silently around the house. Careful to stay hidden while he checks all the windows, he pauses for a second by the front door before turning towards the van with a twisted smile on his face. He motions towards the back of the van and I climb out to figure out what has him tweaked.

Looks like it's game fucking on.

He rounds the back and holds his hand out for his bag. After popping the hatch, he puts the bag down and starts pulling out his 'toys'. I've seen just about everything, but when I see the shit he pulls out, even I get a little jolt of shock. Two railroad spikes, a sledgehammer, duct tape, and a 9mm. I understand the tape and the heat, but the first two throw me.

"Brother, not sure I want to know what you have planned with the spikes and the hammer, but this is your show now. Tell me what to do, where to be, and how to get my boy out."

"For now, the less you know the better. Four total is the count, brother. Heard two bitches yapping and groaning, and another bitch yammering away at the front of the house. You leave them to me. You grab your boy and get the hell outta there. Don't want blowback harming you or your boy. He's gonna need ya. I go in first. You stay right the fuck behind me, man. You duck, you run, I don't give a fuck. Just stay the hell outta my way."

I can work with that. I offer him a nod and follow him to the door. Braxx might sound harsh to some, but I know this is his show, his town, and I want this. I can trust him to get the job done without having a single trail follow me home, and if shit gets hot, he will make sure it cools quickly. Like I said, you don't want him as an enemy, but you can't have better with him as an ally.

The first thing I notice when we burst through the door is the smell. It smells as if this house has been used as a bathroom or mortuary for years. Mixed with the desert heat and no air conditioning, ripe is putting it mildly.

Braxx makes quick work of silencing the bitches that are sitting at the kitchen table snorting lines of coke, and then motions for me to follow the dark hallway towards the back of the house. Even as I move, my limbs start to loosen, my blood starts pumping, and I can feel the adrenaline coursing through my system. Almost as if my body knows that we are in the right place.

The closer I get to the back, the more I can hear the sounds of sex, bodies colliding roughly with the wet smacking of skin, and heavy thumping of what I can only assume is the bedframe banging against the wall. The low moans of a male cause my insides to burn, but when I hear the high-pitched squealing every muscle in my body spasms. I know those fucking squeals.

What the motherfucking hell?!

With a roar powerful enough to shake the foundation, I kick down the door and take in the scene before me. There she is, goddamn Mandy, in all her naked glory doing her best impression of a bucking cowgirl on top of the ugliest son of a bitch I have ever laid eyes on.

Her screams hit my ears, but I only have eyes for the motherfucker under her. He makes quick work of tossing her off his body; I have to fight back the bile when I see his dick spring up between us.

"You! I will fucking deal with you later." I point over at Mandy. Bracing my legs apart and ready to take on anything, I level the man I just know is responsible for taking my girl's mother from this world. With a tone that gives even me the chills, I bite out the only fucking thing I care about. "Where is my son?"

The commotion must have alerted Braxxon because I immediately feel his presence behind me.

"You know this bitch?" He asks, pointing to the side of the room where Mandy is trying to climb to her feet.

"Yeah," I bite but don't get any further when I see the man make his move.

I haven't taken my eyes off the man, still naked, and spitting mad so when he makes to charge me, it isn't hard to block his efforts. My fist connecting with his cheek makes a sickening thunk, and I can hear the bone shatter under the force of my blow. I spare Braxx a quick glance to see him dealing with Mandy. "She stays breathing until I have words, brother," I spit over my shoulder. He gives me a jerk of his chin before dragging her out of the room by her hair.

Moving my full attention back to the other man, I watch as he stumbles slightly, but makes the move to come at me again. This time I don't waste a second. Two quick jabs to his gut have him folding over. Another sharp punch to his temple has him wavering slightly. And when I finally take his head between my hands and slam it down on my raised knee, he crumbles. Blood is coming from his nose, mouth, and ears.

When he finally falls to the floor, I rear back and slam my booted foot into his stomach. "Where is my son, asshole?" I roar in his face.

I get no reply, so I kneel next to his prone form and ask again, "Where the fuck is my son?"

"Fuck… you," he moans.

Wrong answer.

I lose complete sense of reality when my vision goes red, and I light into this motherfucker. It isn't until blood completely covers my hands and I am panting harshly when I'm finally able to pull back, falling to my ass on the blood-covered floor.

I jump slightly when Braxx's menacing growl filled the room. "Brother, you're done. Go, I got this. I'll turn that shit red, Cage. Go"

"I can't find my boy," I say, looking up and meeting Braxx's eyes. Beneath the fury that is taking over his face, I can see the compassion and sorrow for me. "My boy, Braxx."

"Dammit Greg, pull yourself together. Search the entire house, every nook and every fuckin' cranny." His harsh tone sets me straight and I lumber to my feet, shaking off the despair that has started to overtake my system.

I stand from my position on the floor, and pull my shirt over my head to wipe my hands clean. No fucking way I'm touching anything lying around this room.

Besides the trash littering the floor and every available surface, there isn't much in the room. Turning around and getting ready to leave, I notice for the first time a room off to the side. My feet are moving towards the door before I even realize I've had the thought. In my haste, I almost trip over the body Braxx is dragging out of the room in my haste.

Reaching for the knob and finding it locked causes my hope to spark a little. I can't think of any other reason that would have only locked door in this piece of shit.

"COHEN," I scream and pound on the door. "Cohen baby, are you in there?" I listen in silence for a few minutes, my hope slowly dying. "Cohen... son, please be in there."

I am getting ready to knock the door down when I hear a faint sniffle and the one word that can bring my heart back to life. "D-d-daddy?"

"Braxx!" I scream. "I found him"

I try to break the door with my shoulder but it won't budge. The overwhelming need to hold Cohen in my arms, to make sure he is okay, is what is driving me now. "C-Man, I need you to step away from the door. Okay, buddy?" When I hear his soft reply, I step back and kick the door with all my strength, watching it splinter, and pop open. Immediately my eyes start rolling over the small, pitch black room. Before I can even process the whole room, Cohen comes flying into my arms. I pick him up and tuck his head into my shoulder, for the first time since we got the call, feeling that everything is going to be okay.

"Cohen, I need you to close your eyes tight until I say open them, okay? There are some very bad ninjas here that one of my friends is fighting, and I don't want you to see. You understand?" I can feel him nod his head against my shoulder, his tiny body shaking with the force of his sobs and his tears soaking my shirt. "Daddy has you now, Cohen."

I waste no time powering through the house, sparing a quick glance at Braxx and seeing him busy making true on his promise. I doubt there will be one inch of that room that isn't painted red when he is finished.

Only a few hours later, we are camped out in a roach bucket motel room so I can get Cohen cleaned and fed. Braxx has run to the corner store to stock up on some snacks for Cohen while I bathe and change him. Thankfully, in my rush to make it to Vegas, I had the foresight to bring a change of clothes for both of us.

Cohen has passed out in my arms shortly after inhaling every bag of snack food Braxx has brought back. He is out cold, but he is Safe. In. My. Arms.

Even with Cohen here, I won't be able to rest easy without knowing what happened., without knowing that the threat is gone for good. I look up and meet Braxx's gaze. He is waiting for it; he knows me too well and knows I will ask. "Well?"

He looks into my eyes for a few seconds. I can tell he's trying to decide how much to tell me. Whatever he sees in my face must satisfy him. "Bitch number one is taped to a chair, slowly bleedin' out, bro. Long, slow death. Bitch number two... well, that bitch put up a fight, smashed in her skull. Bitch number three is taped to another chair; ain't no way she gettin' loose until my contact picks her up. She was beggin' me to let her go, beggin' for that shit. That cunt is so hung up on you, bro. Obsessed beyond belief. You weren't in the right mind to make that call, brother. You don't want that bitch to make it near your family again. I handled it. Dickhead in there? Well, let's just say he ain't getting up from his chair cause I nailed them spikes through his kneecaps, slit his throat, and bled him dry. You said to turn that shit red, Cage. I turned that shit red." His eyes look tired, but I can tell he is still riding high on adrenaline.

It should be hard hearing that, but these people don't deserve to walk this earth. I promised myself I wouldn't let anyone threaten my family again, and even with the battle of right vs. wrong, I feel like I made the right play.

"What's going to happen to her?" I question. My stomach clenches at just the thought that she could cause more trouble.

"She won't be an issue. My contact has plans for her. She won't ever fuckin' touch your family again." You aren't friends with someone as long as we've been without knowing how to read between the lines. He knows what's eating at me.

I nod my head and look back down at Cohen. "I can't thank you enough for your help, Braxx. I really can't. Next to Melissa, this little boy means the world to me, and you helped get that back. You need something, anything, you call, yeah?

"Will do, brother. Will do." He gives me a nod, his eyes falling on Cohen one more time before pushing off the wall he's leaning against. He takes a few seconds to pull something from his saddlebag and then walks over to the bed. He drops the keys and a fresh license plate on the bed, meets my eyes one last time, and walks out the door. Words aren't necessary at this point. He knows my respect for him runs deep, and I know to a man like Braxxon that my thanks aren't wanted but known.

It is time to take my boy home, get my woman, and pick up the pieces from this fucked up mess.

CHAPTER 27
Greg

I don't waste any time getting the plates switched out and hitting on the road to home. Cohen stirs a few times, and each time ends with his screaming before jolting himself awake. Then when he looks around and sees my face, an instant calm comes over him. Breaks my heart to think about what he's been through, but I have to consider us somewhat lucky that it isn't much, much worse.

About five hours into our drive, I call to check in. Izzy says they had to sedate her again when she realized that I wasn't there. She is hopeful that when she gives her the news that I am on the way back with Cohen that she will be able to regain some sense of reality. Right now, she is too far lost in her grief. It kills to know that she is sitting in a cold hospital room scared, heartbroken, and alone.

When I finally can't stay awake any longer, I pull over somewhere around the middle of Texas. I'm making good time, but it's becoming an issue with our safety if I stay awake. Cohen must be in the same boat as me because he only rouses for a few hours before drifting off again.

I check us into a no-name motel for a few hours. Scooping up Cohen and locking the van, we make our way inside. I lock the door and carry him over to the bed, not even bothering to pull back the sheets. Laying down and tucking him close to my body, I close my arms around him, and seconds later, I am out cold.

When I wake up a few hours later, my mind is hazy, and it takes me a few minutes to remember where I am and why I am there. When I don't feel Cohen immediately, I jolt out of bed in a panic.

Looking around the room, I let out the breath I'm holding when I see him sitting on the end of the bed happily watching TV.

"Cohen," I say on a long exhale.

"Your face looks funny, Daddy." And just like that, I am leveled. Dropping to my knees in front of him, I pull him in tight and just hold him, thanking every God I can think of that he is fine. "Your face is making my neck itchy." He giggles.

"Sorry, little man, hasn't been any time to take care of all my tickle fingers," I joke before rubbing my chin on his little neck.

After we finish laughing, I pull him back and take him in head to toe. "You okay? I know it must have been scary. You're such a brave little man."

He looks at me for a few minutes, his face getting all scrunched up before relaxing, and like nothing has happened, he smiles. "Silly, I knew you would come. You have super powers, remember?"

Of course, super powers.

"That's right. I'll always come." I run my hand through his hair and give him a kiss on his forehead before climbing to my full height. "Alright, sidekick time. All great superheroes have them. Your job is to help me fly our magical van home as quickly as possible. Think you can handle that?"

He jumps off the bed and starts running around animatedly, telling me how we are going to make it home before *SpongeBob* is even over.

He lost me at *SpongeBob*, but I can go with that.

The next fifteen hours of our drive are draining. Cohen is restless, but every time he falls asleep, he wakes back up with a scream. I am starting to worry about what might have happened before I arrived. When I try to talk to him about it, he says that the smelly people made him get in the bathtub, and said if he made any noise, they would hurt his aunt. We don't talk about it after that, but I make a mental note to ask Izzy for the doctor's name that helped her after her run-in with her ex-husband.

When we finally cross over the Georgia border, I have been gone for over three days. Three days that I needed to be home. Three days that my woman has been suffering without me.

The last check in from Izzy has left me feeling a lot better. She told me that she is with Melissa at our house and she is dealing much better. She still has moments when she will break down, but for the most part, she seems oddly hyper and very obviously waiting on our return.

It is pushing close to late afternoon when we finally pull into town. I have Maddox and Coop meet me at the town line with my truck so that they can dispose of the van while I get home to Melissa. No fucking way I am risking everything by driving that van right up to the door. I am going to have a hard enough time just explaining how I happen to show up with the child everyone is looking for.

My wheels haven't even crossed the end of the driveway when I see her. Flying through the front door, she is running as fast as she can across the yard to reach the truck. The second she opened that front door, I stop the truck and get out so when she reached me, crashing into my body with enough force to almost knock me to my knees, I am ready.

I will always be ready.

She doesn't speak; she just holds me with a bone crushing force. After a minute of her holding on and letting out all her grief, she pulls back and stares into my eyes. I'm sure mine are just as red rimmed and wet as hers. No need to hold it in now. The pressure, stress, worry, and heartbreak from the last few days just roll off me. The adrenaline that I have been running on vanishes the second I hold her in my arms.

"He's really okay?" She asks, running her small hands over my cheeks, through my beard, and down my chest, as if she is assessing me for injuries of some sort.

"He's really okay, Beauty. Having trouble sleeping unless he is holding my hand or I'm holding him, but he's really okay."

"You?" Her hands are still roaming over my body. When she gets to my hands and sees the damage to my knuckles, she doesn't ask. She just brings my hands to her lips and starts crying again.

"Melissa, look at me." I wait until she calms down and brings her eyes up to mine. "I need you to rally it together, pull that strength that I know you have together, and help me. I want to fall apart too, baby, but right now, we need to pull it together for our boy, yeah?"

She takes a few deep breaths and nods her head. She has to visibly collect herself when we start the walk to Cohen's side of the truck.

"He's been awake since Mississippi, finally crashed somewhere mid-Alabama, but he's okay." We stand there and take him in. Safe and sound.

His lips pucker slightly in his sleep, but every few seconds, they curl up in a smile. His light brown hair is a crazy mess, and his clothes have various food stains over every inch of fabric. But right now, right now, he couldn't look anymore perfect.

That night, I have to deal with reporting that Cohen is home. It is a damn good thing that I have such a close relationship with almost every cop, detective, and P.I in the area. They don't ask many questions when I tell them that I am the one who found him. Well, one of them did, but Maddox stepped in, and with a shake of his head, the rookie cop shut his mouth. The child is safe and that is what it all boils down too. I did have one pull me aside as he was leaving to ask if he should still be looking for Susan Wagner and her partner. I don't say a word, but he would be a fucking idiot to miss the look that I give him.

I brief the guys on what has happened, and let them fill in the blanks.

As I was leaving for Vegas, Maddox started doing what he is best at. He sat down in his room full of computers and searched until he found the trail.

When Mandy had begun to realize that I really was done with her, she became obsessed with breaking up Melissa and me. She had made it her personal mission to find out everything she could about us. It wasn't hard to see that she had been stalking Melissa for months. When Coop went to her apartment, she had walls and walls of pictures. Some of Melissa, some of me, some of Cohen, but the majority were ones with three of us together. The only difference was that she had put *her* face over Melissa's. She had created this whole fantasy life where we were going to live happily ever after with our little boy.

Disgusted doesn't even come close to how I feel about that. We have all agreed that it is best to mention that to no one.

We still aren't clear on the how, but she had hooked up with Susan and hired the man we later identified as Bruno Clark to snatch Cohen. They didn't seem to have a set plan after that, because the trail ended in Vegas.

When I found out just how sick Mandy was, I was glad she was rotting somewhere deep in the bowels of Vegas. I struggled with not knowing for sure what happened to her. In the end, I had to call Braxx. His answer was to leave it be and just know that bitch wouldn't touch my family again. She was gone and I'm pretty fucking sure it was best I didn't know where she ended up. Sure bet, it was a living hell on earth.

The first few nights home are rough. We sit down and explain to Cohen that his Nana got her wings, and now she is going to sit in the clouds and watch over him. He handles it as well as a three-year-old can, but later in the day, when he gets tired, he starts asking for Nana again. Melissa has to leave the room because she doesn't want him to see her breakdown, but I know that's what is happening.

After another talk about angels and heaven, he seems to understand a little better.

That night, he falls asleep between us.

The next night is a little easier but he still isn't able to leave our bed.

It isn't until another week after the funeral that he is finally able to sleep in his own bed.

Melissa is doing better. She has her moments but she usually excuses herself when they happen. A few times, I find her in the shower, or sitting deep in the closet falling into herself, but I am able to talk her around.

Bottom line is that no one in my house is handling the situation well. It isn't until another week has passed that I remember Izzy's psychologist. She specializes in grief and PTSD, and has helped both Izzy and myself after I almost lost my life trying to save hers. It doesn't take any convincing to get Melissa on board. She knows that we aren't going to heal until we talk to someone, express our loss, our fears, and everything in between.

That is the first day that I see some life come back into her eyes. That is when I know that we will be okay, that we will get past this.

Melissa

I don't remember much from the days following my mother's murder. I remember waking up a few times and seeing Izzy, or one of the guys. I remember crying for Cohen and crying for Greg, but for the most part, the days that followed are blank. I don't want to remember those days when the pain was so raw I feared it would consume me. I didn't want to remember the fear that consumed me when I thought I would never see Cohen again, never get to listen to him go on and on about ninjas or wieners. And I don't want to think about what I felt when I thought I was going to lose Greg too.

I do remember what it felt like when I watched his truck pull into the driveway, and I saw his face and the shadow of my sleeping little man in the backseat. I do remember the head-to-toe reaction that my body had when Greg stepped out of the truck and I fell into his arms.

When Izzy told me he was on his way home with Cohen, I knew without a doubt that there was nothing this man wouldn't do if he felt it was best for his family.

We don't talk about the details of his trip to bring Cohen home. I don't want to know. What we do talk about now is how lucky we are. We have been given a chance that few in our position ever have. A second chance at life.

CHAPTER 28
Melissa

It's been two month since we lost my mom and almost lost Cohen. Today we are going out to celebrate my twenty-ninth birthday. The plans aren't really anything special, but it's just another way we are staying on our path back to normal.

Cohen is almost back to the little boy he was before all of this. He still has days that he will ask for my mom, but now that his time is filled with constant Greg bonding, he is finally moving on.

"Melissa?" I've been in the bathroom getting ready for the last fifteen minutes. He's lucky that it doesn't take me years to get ready, but my men are ready to eat so they don't mind rushing me.

"In here, babe!" I call out the door before returning to the mirror to finish applying my mascara.

"You almost ready?" he asks and bends to kiss my temple. "Cohen is ready, cape and all."

Of course he is. One of these days, he might take that thing off but right now, it might as well be surgically attached.

"Almost." I cap the mascara and turn, fisting his shirt and pulling him towards me. When my lips meet his,

I run my hands up his solid chest before pushing my fingers into his hair. He hums his approval into my mouth and just like that, we forget the world around us.

When he grabs my ass and pulls me to his body, I know I accidently woke the beast. Pulling away, offer him a look of regret before speaking, "Sorry, I really just wanted a kiss before we left."

"Happy to accommodate you Beauty, but let's make sure the next time you want a kiss like that, that we aren't about to go meet up with the gang to have dinner. Sitting around for hours and shooting the shit is no fun when my dick is about to be strangled by my pants." I start to laugh and turn to walk out into the bedroom, almost knocking Cohen over in the process.

"Daddy? What's a dick and why are your pants hurting him?" I turn back and look at Greg. His face is open with astonishment and his cheeks have a little color on them. Who would have thought that it's actually possible to shock the man.

"Um, C-Man, remember that day I told you there were some questions you can't ask until you're ten?" He waits for Cohen's little head to nod before continuing, "Well, that is one of those questions you can't ask again until then, okay?"

"That's okay, Daddy. I'll just ask Maddox Locke!" Ever since Cohen got back from Vegas, Greg can't stand the thought of putting him in pre-school. He just feels like it's too soon. So Cohen has become the newest member of the Corps Security team. Since those men have a tendency to go by last names, first names, both, or sometimes neither, Cohen was slightly confused with what he should call them. He finally decided to call them whatever he wanted. Not everyone got both first and last names. He seemed to save this for his favorites only.

Beck is now Beckett. Maddox is Maddox Locke, and my personal favorite, Sway is Dilbert.

"Good idea. Ask him." Greg makes quick work in ushering Cohen out of the room so I can continue to get ready. I am still laughing when I make my way downstairs to meet up with my boys.

It doesn't take long to get to the restaurant. We have decided to meet up at one of the local Italian places that we all enjoy, and as normal, we are the last to arrive. One of these days, we will be first, maybe. Probably not.

When we walk in, I am immediately ambushed. I get a smile from Greg before he takes Cohen by the hand and leads him to the table. When Izzy, Dee, and Emmy finally shove me into the bathroom, the questions started flying.

"What the hell?" flies from Izzy.

"Would have been nice to get a call! Is that too much to ask?" sputters Dee.

"Did he knock you up?" Surprisingly, this comes from Emmy.

We all look over at her and I laugh when her ivory cheeks instantly flush. "What?" she whispers. "You were all thinking it too."

I laugh outright with that comment. Truth is, this is something I knew was coming. Greg and I have already talked about what would happen if we did it. The backlash we, or rather I, will have to deal with. It looks like he was right. My girlfriends don't like the thought that they have missed our wedding. But, I know, it's more than that. Izzy and Greg are like family, so for us to disappear and run up to the mountains for a quick wedding with just him, Cohen, and me, well, it isn't sitting well with Izzy.

"I'm sorry?" I offer. "Actually I'm not, but you can believe that if it makes you feel better." They all laugh, but I can tell that Izzy is still a little sour.

"I wish I could have been there. I'm so happy for you two, but I wish I could have seen him get married." I understand where she is coming from. And so does Greg. But, this is about us and that's what really mattered.

"I know, Iz. I really do, but we needed this. It was something special for us. It was just a small ceremony with us and Cohen, then later we had a special day to do things our sisters and my mother would have enjoyed." And we did. We did small things like drop feathers down one of the mountains that we hiked up, watching them as they floated away. We even found a wishing well. These little things will mean something to Cohen one day.

"So that means you aren't knocked up?" Dee asks hopefully.

"No, I'm not knocked up." I laugh when her face falls. "Not now, but we aren't doing anything to prevent it. If it happens, it does. It's just one of those things we've let go of the control on and now, we're just living our lives."

"Well, I'm happy for you," Emmy offers and wraps her small arms around me.

"I am too. I promise. I was a little upset about it, but I understand." Izzy smiles and her green eyes twinkle with moisture. "You're kind of like my sister now." She steps forward and gives me a hug. I haven't thought about it that way, but she's right. I think, and not for the first time in the last few months, how truly blessed I am.

"What's your problem?" I hear Emmy ask Dee. "You're this disappointed that she isn't knocked up?"

She looks at us for a while, taking her time to look us all in the eye. Crazy chick really is disappointed and is doing a shit job at hiding it.

"What? So what if I'm a little upset. I was looking forward to having another baby around here now that Nate is all 'alpha baby'."

"What the hell is an alpha baby?" Izzy asks on a laugh.

"Uh, really? He is constantly saying 'mine'. But does he say it about normal things a one year old would claim? Noooo, not Axel Reid's baby. His baby claims boobs, Izzy. I took him with me to the mall the other day, and when we ran into Victoria's Secret to get some new boyshorts, because hey, they were on sale so why not? Anyway, we walk in and he starts pointing to every mannequin, every sales lady's chest. Then when I'm checking out, he pulls my top down and screams 'mine'. You have issues with that boy if he is already chasing tits at one."

Before she is even halfway through her story, we're all wiping the tears away and laughing like loons. Jesus, sometimes the things that come out of her mouth are just unbelievable.

"Did you ever think that maybe he was just hungry?" Izzy asks. Like just the thought of her breast fed child being hungry might not even be on Dee's radar.

"No. I didn't, because it's just weird you are still breastfeeding and your child has teeth. What if he bites off your nipple?"

"You're serious?" Emmy says in shock.

"Hell yes, I am. When I have kids, there is no way they are coming anywhere near my girls with teeth. No way."

"You're ridiculous, it's good for him. And seriously, Dee, I had them pierced. Do you really think a nip here and there is going to bother these milk machines?" I can tell that Izzy is starting to get upset. This is a debate we have constantly, 'we' being Dee against us. There is just no turning her around on that whole teeth and nipples thing.

"Gah! Can you not call them milk machines?" Dee shrieks.

"You know Dee, I don't know what you're so freaked out about. I love it when Greg uses his teeth." I laugh when her jaw drops. It really is just too easy to shock her these days. I'm pretty sure the last time she got some, Bush Sr. was president.

"I do not need to know that about Greg." She looks over at Izzy who is still laughing. "Why are you laughing? That's just gross?"

Izzy calms herself down, and looks at Dee with mirth dancing in her bright eyes. "Then I guess you don't want to hear her tell you about when she first discovered he has not one, not two, but three piercings on his junk!" She starts laughing all over again when Dee starts gagging and leaves the bathroom.

"Cruel, but fucking hilarious." I laugh right along with Izzy for a few seconds. When we both are able to stop, I look at her and offer a small smile. "Are you really okay? I know you wanted to be there with us, but this really was just something that we needed to do, just the three of us."

"My feelings were hurt for a second, but then Axel explained it to me. I understand, really I do." We hug for a second before she pulls back and grabs my hand. "At least he did something right."

She's not wrong there either. While he and Emmy take turns complimenting the ring he picked out for me, I take a second to take it all in again.

My heart swells when I think about what wearing these rings mean. My *husband*. It's so new, and honestly hasn't sunk in yet. Not sure that it even will for a while, but the thought that the man I was so determined to avoid and evade is now my husband and soon the adoptive father of Cohen, makes my heart expand.

When we make it back to the table, Greg stands and pulls the chair out for me. Right as I'm getting ready to say hey to Beck sitting at my right, Greg leans over and whispers in my ear. "Do you know why Dee came out before you three spouting some nonsense about me being disgusting?" I look across the table at Dee. She is still looking at Greg as if he's the carrier of every incurable disease out there, and it has me in fits all over again.

"Knock it off, Dee!" I yell across the table.

She shakes her head a few times and looks back at Greg, "There are just some things that I do not want to know about you. Three? Really?"

Greg wraps his arm around my shoulder and pulls me closer to his side. I can feel his laughter vibrating through his shaking body as he laughs at Dee. With my husband's strong arms wrapped around me, Cohen in his lap, and all of our friends surrounding us, I thank my sister for the millionth time for always reminding me to live.

We decide to leave dinner a little early. When Izzy asks if Cohen can spend the night at their house, a very excited three-year-old yelps 'yes' across the table, and Greg doesn't waste any time paying the tab, and dragging me out of the restaurant.

"You're acting like a beast, Greg." I laugh, struggling to keep up with his long legged strides.

"Told you, every Beauty needs her Beast, and your beast was just guaranteed a whole night of uninterrupted sex with his wife. So let's move, woman." When I still can't keep up with his stomping strides towards the truck, he spins, and before I have a chance to protest, he puts his shoulder in my gut and I am hanging over his back.

"Greg!" I can't even fake outrage at this point. This is my man and I fucking love it.

When we reach the truck, he all but throws me in the seat. He does take the time to lean into my body and devour my lips in a soul-consuming kiss full of promise off what is to come. When he pulls away, I whimper and he laughs.

"Yeah, you feel me now."

"Beast."

The car ride home is full of thick heat. Not because of the temperature, but because we both know we may make it two steps into the house, if lucky, before coming together.

Ever since Cohen has come to live with us full time, we have had to become creative with our sex life. The time he pushed me into the pantry and gave me the hottest five minutes between our can goods is one of my favorites. Almost getting busted by Cohen was not. I am convinced that that kid came with a built-in cockblocker. If anything, having the little guy around just makes us hotter for each other when we are able to steal time away together.

Then again, with Greg Cage, every time feels like the first time.

When we pull into the neighborhood, offering Stan a wave, and make our way to the house, I unbuckle my belt and prepare for what will come next. Predictable as always, he pulls right up to the front door, climbs out, and stalks over to my door. At least this time he cradles me in his arms bridal style as he storms to the door. I reach out and take care of the locks, and in two seconds, we are in the door with it shut, and locked, and my back flat against the cold steel.

"Can't wait, Beauty," he said against my lips. "Need to feel you. Need to love you."

"Don't want to wait," I reply and start to help him pull clothes off. We trip, crashing to the floor. Before we hit, he rolls so his body takes the brunt of impact.

We're a blur of clothing and limbs as we rush to connect. Sometimes I feel that moments like this are our way of reminding each other that we are both alive, that we have both have overcome and are still here, living our lives and loving hard.

"Love you," I tell him, leaning forward, and looking down our bodies to watch him guide his dick into my pussy. I grab both his thick pecs and start moving against him. My favorite piercing adds the perfect friction against my clit.

I feel his hands start gliding up my stomach before he cups my breasts, and starts rolling and pinching my nipples. My head rolls back on my shoulders and I start to move faster, enjoying one of the rare times he allows me to stay on top.

After I start to falter in my movement some, he grabs my hips and starts lifting me up, and slamming my body down, meeting me thrust for thrust, and glide for glide. Our moans dance together, and when I feel myself start to unravel, I lean forward slightly, waiting for him to curl up and meet my lips.

And right there, a tangle of limbs and our lips locked together, we both reach our release at the same time. Completely connected. Mind, body, and soul.

Living the life we are blessed to have.

Beauty and her Beast.

Epilogue

"I haven't been here for months. I could blame the weather but winter ended weeks ago. I could blame work, but you would both know that I would be lying through my teeth. I could blame a number of things, but the only truth is I have been afraid. It's one thing to come with the boys. With them around, I can't breakdown and I can pretend that you're both still here." I sigh deeply and lay down on the cool grass. "I had to come this time. I wanted to be the one to tell you both. I wanted you two to be the first people I told. I haven't even told Greg or Cohen yet, although I have a feeling when I do, they will celebrate so loudly you will still hear them."

I look up into the cloudless sky with a smile and continue with my reason for coming, "It only took six months, but the adoption paperwork came today. Greg and I are officially Cohen's legal parents. Cohen thinks it's cool that he's getting a new name. Cohen Cage. He says it is a better superhero name." I laugh a few times before sobering.

"I wish you were both still here. I always thought of this moment and each time, I would have you both here with me. But just like we tell Cohen, I know you're still up there and happy for me."

It takes me a few minutes before I can speak past the lump in my throat. "I went to the doctor today," I whisper, "I hope it's a girl, Fia. Remember all those times we would talk about how amazing it would be to have a son first and then a daughter so they would always have protection? I can't wait to watch Cohen become a brother." I lay there for a few more moments with a smile on my face and think back to all the times we planned our future. It gets easier, missing my family, but never stops hurting.

"I miss you guys. I just wanted to let you know, let you be the first to know, that Cohen is okay and that pretty soon, our family will grow. Wish so hard you were here to share this with me. I love you, mom. I love you, Fia."

I climb to my feet and take one more look at the two gravestones that mark my family.

I love you two, so, so much.

When I drive home from the cemetery, I feel that pressure of grief ease off my heart and soar into the sky for the first time since I lost Fia.

When I pull into the driveway and see my husband and our son rolling around in the grass, I know that even through the heartache and pain, we have both learned to fly.

We have lived.

And now we can teach our children how to do the same thing.

~ THE END ~

The Corps Security series will continue with Beck & Dee's story.

Continue reading for a peek into book 3, Beck.

Prologue

"Denise, you need to stop this nonsense. A girl at your age needs to show some maturity and stop being so needy. You are perfectly capable of keeping yourself occupied. This is a big night for your father; you could try and be a little supportive." She turns her perfectly painted face back to the mirror, applying more of her make-up. I always wondered how she was able to get all that make-up on when her face never really moves. Her weekly appointments to the spa take care of the winkles that I've never been able to find.

"But Mother, tonight's my chorus recital at school." I whisper meekly. Even at thirteen, I know I should stand up for myself but I just can't seem to do that with my mother, the ice queen. "How am I supposed to get there?"

Before I can react, her hand cracks against my cheek. "Don't be such an ungrateful brat, Denise. Some children can only dream of living the life we have given you. I don't want to hear another word from you tonight. Go on up to your room."

Blinking back the wetness that rushes to my eyes, I back up slowly, keeping my eyes trained on my mother. I don't realize I have been holding my breath until I bump into the hard, unforgiving body standing behind me.

"What have you done now, Denise?" My father's deep baritone rumbles through the room. A cold ribbon of fear snakes down my back. I brace myself for his anger as I turn to face him.

"I'm sorry, Father. I just wanted to ask Mother about my chorus recital. I'm supposed to be at the school in an hour." I don't dare break eye contact with my father. No one would dare. He demands your full attention and respect. I will give him my attention, but before I started middle school, I learned he didn't deserve my respect.

"You stupid little girl. I've told you, extracurricular activities should be things that can further your career. Things like *chorus* aren't going to take you on the path to greatness. First thing Monday, I want you to speak with your teachers about dropping that."

My insides seize, because I knew better than to even mention the recital, and I still did it. I should have just faked a sickness Monday at school. For the last year, I've been successful in keeping my 'fun time' from my parents. They don't care what I am doing. They don't want me, so they've never even noticed.

"Am I understood, Denise?" His tone has a sharper edge to it and I know this is not a point to drag my feet on.

"Yes, Sir," I reply. "May I be excused?" I just want to get away. Away from their room, them, and this life they say I should be grateful for. Who would be grateful for this? Two parents that don't want you. All the money in the world, but no happiness? I would rather be living in the slums.

Walking as quickly as possible, I make quick work of the maze of hallways and enter my room. Only when the door closes do I let out my breath and let my body relax. Ever since I've been old enough to know the difference, I've known my parents don't like me. No, they don't just 'not like' me... they hate me. I am the accident that should have been terminated, or so they remind me often enough. I don't even think my mother cares either way. She just wants the life my father has given her, regardless of the fact that even her own daughter knows he is sleeping with the hired help.

And my father? My father is the reason that I know you can never trust a boy. Never allow one into your heart. They only care about one thing and one thing only. Themselves. Every man in my life has let me down. My grandfather died before he was successful in taking me away from my parents. My father is as evil as they come. And just today, my boyfriend Toby said he wanted to go out with Malinda 'I have bigger boobs than my eighteen-year-old sister' Monroe.

There will never be a boy in the world that can make me forget that the only person I can count on is me. I can't wait to get away from this place. The day I turn eighteen, I am running as fast as I can. I've made sure that I get good grades, and that I will have my pick of schools to choose from. Because the first day I leave this hell, I am going to be a new person. I am going to be happy. I am going to be loved. And I am going to find people to share my life with that want to be around me.

But I will never, ever trust a boy.

Add this to your Good Reads TBR list by clicking here:

http://www.goodreads.com/book/show/18069234-beck